"Let me up!"

Kirby laughed, trying to push Matt off. But he tumbled her onto her back in the snow, then covered her with the entire length of his massive body. Kirby's hormones simmered in response, and she fully expected the snow to melt beneath her.

"First you have to say 'uncle,' " Matt responded.

Playing like children, they tussled in the snow—until Matt's fingers brushed over Kirby's breasts in an attempt to capture her hands.

An accident? she wondered, suddenly so distracted that he actually succeeded and pinned her wrists to his racing heart.

"Say 'uncle.' "

"What if I refuse?" she asked breathlessly.

"I'll be forced to hold you here forever," he replied.

"Sweet temptation . . ." Only when Matt tensed did Kirby realize she'd uttered her crazy thought aloud. . . .

Dear Reader,

The festive season is often so hectic—a whirlwind of social calls, last-minute shopping, wrapping, baking, tree decorating and finding that perfect hiding place for the children's gifts! But it's also a time to pause and reflect on the true meaning of the holiday: love, peace and goodwill.

Silhouette Romance novels strive to bring the message of love all year round. Not just the special love between a man and woman, but the love for children, family and the community, in stories that capture the laughter, the tears and, *always,* the happy-ever-afters of romance.

I hope you enjoy this month's wonderful love stories—including our WRITTEN IN THE STARS selection, *Arc of the Arrow* by Rita Rainville. And in months to come, watch for Silhouette Romance titles by your all-time favorites, including Diana Palmer, Brittany Young and Annette Broadrick.

The authors and editors of Silhouette Romance books wish you and your loved ones the very best of the holiday season . . . and don't forget to hang the mistletoe!

Sincerely,

Valerie Susan Hayward
Senior Editor

LINDA VARNER

Mistletoe and Miracles

Silhouette Romance

Published by Silhouette Books New York

America's Publisher of Contemporary Romance

To each and every friend who read my hurriedly
typed, lined out, penciled over pages and told me
they were good. You know who you are. I thank you all.

SILHOUETTE BOOKS
300 E. 42nd St., New York, N.Y. 10017

MISTLETOE AND MIRACLES

ISBN: 0-373-08835-3

First Silhouette Books printing December 1991

Books by Linda Varner

Silhouette Romance

Heart of the Matter #625
Heart Rustler #644
Luck of the Irish #665
Honeymoon Hideaway #698
Better to Have Loved #734
A House Becomes a Home #780
Mistletoe and Miracles #835

LINDA VARNER

has always had a vivid imagination. For that reason, while most people counted sheep to get to sleep, she made up romances. The search for a happy ending sometimes took more than one night, and when one story grew to mammoth proportions, Linda decided to write it down. The result was her first romance novel.

Happily married to her junior high school sweetheart, Linda, the mother of two and a full-time secretary, still finds that the best time to plot her latest project is late at night when the house is quiet and she can create without interruption. Linda lives in Conway, Arkansas, where she was raised, and believes the support of her family, friends and writers' group made her dream to be published come true.

SNOWBALL COOKIES

1 cup soft margarine
½ cup confectioners' sugar
1 tsp vanilla
2¼ cups flour
¼ tsp salt
¾ cup finely chopped pecans
Additional confectioners' sugar for coating

Preheat oven to 400° F.

Cream together margarine, confectioners' sugar and vanilla. Blend thoroughly. Add flour and salt. Blend well. Mix in pecans. Chill dough in refrigerator for 10 minutes.

Roll dough into 1″ balls. Place on ungreased cookie sheet. It is all right to put these fairly close together since they don't spread as they bake.

Bake 10 to 12 minutes, until set but not brown. Roll in confectioners' sugar while still warm. Let cookies cool completely. Roll them in the sugar again.

Makes 4 dozen cookies.

Chapter One

"Not far now," Kirby Gibson said with as much enthusiasm as she could muster. Her car wasn't fooled for a moment and coughed ominously in the thin mountain air. Its windshield wipers beat a staccato rhythm in their fight against the blinding snowstorm, keeping time to the music on the radio.

Kirby reached to turn down the volume, as though that would help her see better. Anxiously she scanned the dense Wyoming forest on either side of the road. Then her gaze darted ahead in search of the elusive turn that would take her to shelter and warmth.

Kirby thought back to the last time she'd been to "Gibson Ridge," as the site of her grandmother's three-room cabin was called by the locals. So much had happened since that visit almost a year ago. So very much. Her younger sister, Madison, had mar-

ried Jason Lawrence and moved to New York; their
beloved grandmother had died; Kirby had begun her
career as a consultant for Time is Money, Inc....

Shaking her head in wonder at the changes in her
life, Kirby squinted through the ice-smeared glass and
the gray of dusk. She saw nothing but the winding
highway and trees, trees, trees. Beautiful trees they
were, too—tall pines, frosted with snow, garnished
with icicles. Any other time she would have cherished
the sight or stopped to take a picture. Today she had
more pressing issues on her mind.

"Maybe coming up here alone wasn't such a brilliant idea, after all," Kirby murmured when she
rounded yet another curve without spotting the expected road.

Then suddenly there it was—the narrow pathway to
Christmas, past and present. A quick peek through
snow-laden limbs confirmed her words and revealed
the rustic log-and-stone dwelling willed to her and
Madison by their grandmother. Kirby sighed her relief, maneuvered the tricky turn and carefully covered
the remaining distance to her haven.

Moments later she stomped through the ankle-deep
snow to the front porch of the cabin that was such a
delightful blend of the old and the new. She noted with
pleasure that some wood lay stacked on the porch and
sighed wistfully, already picturing herself stretched out
in front of the double-sided fireplace, which provided
heat to both the bedroom and living room. She could
almost feel the warmth of the blaze, smell the pun-
gent smoke....

Quickly Kirby freed a hand to unlock the door and then flicked on the light as soon as she stepped inside. The cabin felt oddly warm, a fact she attributed to chilled cheeks, half-frozen fingers and damp hair. That did not explain the absence of musty, dusty odor one could expect on entering a deserted residence, or the lived-in feeling that was almost like a presence.

Although slightly spooked, Kirby credited her uncharacteristic nervousness to an overactive imagination. Any "presence" in this cabin could only be a friendly one. The years spent here with her grandmother had been wonderful...special. This visit would be just the same, if a little lonelier.

Humming "Have Yourself a Merry Little Christmas," to boost her flagging spirits, she dumped her load on the sofa and looked around. At first glance everything appeared to be exactly as it had the last time she was there: split-log floors, hand-hewn walls, exposed rafters. A closer inspection revealed clutter—something an everything-in-its-place woman like Kirby abhorred. She saw books and papers stacked everywhere, what could only be a man's sweater and jeans draped over an arm of the couch and two pairs of men's shoes lying on the floor next to the recliner.

"How like Jason to leave the place a mess," she grumbled aloud before heading back outside into the elements. And what elements they were. The snowstorm had increased in fury and showed every sign of being exactly what the weatherman had predicted—a record breaker. Kirby didn't mind. In fact, she was counting on it and had come prepared.

More important, she'd shared her holiday plans with her sister and an old suitor of her grandmother, Walter Williams, who owned the country store five miles to the south. Walter had promised to check on her every few days via radio, and Kirby knew that he had a four-wheel-drive truck by which to stage a rescue if the solitude got to be too much. That wasn't going to happen, of course. Kirby intended to have a marvelous time so she could brag to her sister, who'd chosen to spend Christmas with Jason's family in Vermont.

As quickly as possible, Kirby grabbed up the rest of the supplies. But her teeth still chattered by the time she leapt back onto the porch and dashed inside. She picked up a split log that already lay by the fireplace—no doubt another leftover from the weekend Jason and Madison had spent there a few months ago—and tossed it on top of the charred remains of an earlier blaze. With the flick of a match, she set fire to it . . . or tried to. It didn't ignite at once, and a frustrating ten minutes passed before Kirby sat back and eyed the dubious beginnings of what she hoped would be a roaring fire.

After shedding her stylish fake-fur jacket, she surveyed the hodgepodge of essentials she'd brought, intending to get started on putting them away. But it was Friday night of an exhausting week, and she was going to be at the cabin until after the New Year—ten whole days. Surely tomorrow would be soon enough to unpack the imperishable groceries. The perishables were carefully iced down in an insulated chest. There was no reason she couldn't get out of her clothes and into a hot shower before she dealt with them.

Now humming "White Christmas," Kirby opened her suitcase to extract her nightie and a bar of her favorite scented soap. She then made a beeline through the darkened bedroom to the bath. In no time she stood under a cascade of steamy water. Heaven, she decided, relishing the moment. Pure heaven. There was nothing more relaxing than a . . .

. . . *hot shower, that's what I need,* Dillion Mathias Foxx told himself as he shouldered his camera case and tripod. Head ducked against the whipping wind, Matt trudged the remaining distance to the back door of the old cabin he'd occupied the past eight weeks. He skirted his faithful old pickup truck, almost hidden under a drift of snow, and climbed the steps into the kitchen, only to halt abruptly when he noticed the light on in the living room.

The cabin had been dark when he'd headed out that morning . . . hadn't it? The goose bumps skittering down Matt's spine said yes. Common sense told him differently.

"Relax," Matt softly scolded himself as he slipped out of his jacket and draped it over the back of one of the two chairs still pushed up to the table. With trembling fingers, he combed through his hair, badly in need of a cut, then smoothed the beard he hadn't quite gotten used to. "You're a little jumpy, that's all. You've been writing intrigue and assassination for two months now and you've got murder on the brain."

Writing? Ha. So far he'd skied, chopped wood, hiked, taken photographs, paced and slept. Jason Lawrence, his publisher, was going to kill him when he found out, especially since he'd loaned Matt this little hidey-hole on the sole condition that another Matt Foxx thriller would be on his desk in New York by Christmas—three days and ten chapters away.

Shaking his head with regret at this unfortunate and uncharacteristic bout of writer's block, Matt headed out of the kitchen to the living room. But just inside the door, he halted again. In the fireplace lay dying embers, and on the floor at the foot of the built-in bunk beds were boxes and bundles of every shape and size.

Obviously he'd had a visitor while he was out. But who? he wondered, now more baffled than worried. It was a few days too early for Saint Nick to stop by, and thieves generally *took* things instead of leaving them.

At that moment the sound of singing, soprano and a little off-key, filled the air. Matt almost jumped out of his skin. A second later he recognized the tune and relaxed again. A thief with the holiday spirit? That sounded more like one of the characters in the Dillon Mathias children's books he secretly wrote. Well, thief or whatever, her dreams were about to come true. This godforsaken mountain was definitely, but definitely, going to have a white Christmas.

When the singing became soft humming, curiosity got the best of Matt, who cautiously peeked into the shadowy bedroom. Since he heard water running, he surmised that someone—a female someone—now showered in his bathroom next door. Amazing.

And darned intriguing. Fearless now, Matt crept on into the bedroom, which smelled of springtime—specifically, honeysuckle. The light streaming through the open bathroom door illuminated a trail of clothes on the floor. As quietly as possible, since the water had now been turned off, he headed to the bath, sidestepping the clothes and one—one?—leather boot. His gaze shifted to the bed, where he spied a nightgown and a pair of bikini panties laid out and waiting....

Bikini panties? Grinning his delight, Matt picked up the wisp of pink lace, which he eyed with avid curiosity. No burglar, this. At least he didn't think so. More like Goldilocks... all grown-up.

Would she settle for a Foxx instead of a bear? he wondered with a hopeful glance toward the bathroom. At this point he was so desperate for an excuse not to write that he'd almost welcome a visit from a female, even one of the money-hungry variety who'd sent him into hiding in the first place.

Almost...

Though tempted to barge right on into the bathroom, Matt decided to do the noble thing and retreat to the living room to wait for his "guest." Absently twirling the panties on his finger, he turned to exit but froze when a board creaked loudly under his foot. Next door the yuletide solo abruptly ceased.

"Who's there?" a female voice demanded with obvious trepidation. There was a long silence, during which Matt held his breath and didn't move a muscle. "Is anybody out there?" The last words came in a singsong that seemed to say the owner of that lilting voice did not really expect a reply. Matt next heard soft laughter, then disconcertingly close to the connecting door, ''Kirby Lee Gibson, you are such a weenie-E-E-E!''

That earsplitting screech told Matt that she'd spotted him. Cramming the panties into his pocket, he whirled to confront this Kirby Lee Gibson, who promptly threw something at him. Matt ducked...too late. The missing boot hit him square on the chest.

Yelping, Matt did the only thing he could do: leap and grab. Only when he held Kirby's squirming body in his arms did he realize she wore nothing but a towel...and wasn't really wearing that.

He jumped back reflexively. The woman, a petite blonde, wasted not a moment, but gave him a swift kick in the knee and then darted back into the bathroom. The walls reverberated with the slam of the door. The lock clicked with finality.

Matt barely registered the sound. Groaning his agony, he flexed his injured knee to see if it were still functional. It was...barely. Matt hobbled to the door and tried the knob before banging loudly on it with his fist. ''Lady, I want to talk to you.''

She did not respond.

''Hey in there!''

Matt heard a rasping screak that told him she'd raised the window in the bathroom. His jaw dropped. Surely she wasn't climbing outside...in her birthday suit...in twenty-degree weather.

Born crazy? Matt wondered. Or just scared out of her wits?

Probably the latter, he decided ruefully. He'd apparently given her as big a shock as she'd given him. And though she had no right to take refuge in his cabin—for whatever reason—he couldn't turn her out with wet hair and bare feet. Without further thought, Matt limped back outside the way he'd come in, intent on putting her fears to rest.

By the time he rounded the corner of the building, she dangled several feet above the ground by her fingertips, her back to him. Matt noted with mixed emotions that the long johns he hadn't been able to find anywhere that morning now encased her slender body.

As unwilling to frighten her as to let her put her bare toes on the snow, Matt slowed and then halted in a quandary of indecision. Obviously unaware of him, she twisted her neck to peer down below, as though judging the drop to the ground. Matt took immediate advantage of her hesitation, rushing forward just in time to catch her just when she released the window ledge.

She screamed when his arms slipped around her waist—screamed, squirmed and kicked his knee again...hard. He stumbled but somehow managed to hold on. "If you kick me again, I swear I'm going to dump you right here in the snow—bare feet or no."

Dump her? Her captor wanted to *dump her?* Kirby frowned in confusion and momentarily halted her efforts to escape. "Does that mean you're not going to ravage me?"

He made a choking sound. "Right at this moment that's the last thing on my mind. But don't press your luck."

"Press my luck?"

"Wiggle," he qualified.

Kirby blushed clear to her half-frozen toes. At once intensely aware of the thin thermal underwear and her backside rubbing against his manly front, she ceased her struggles altogether.

"That's better," he said, his husky voice right in her ear. "Now turn just a little and put your arm around my neck...that's right...."

Amazingly Kirby found herself helping him readjust their positions so that he carried her as a groom would carry his bride en route to their threshold. But unlike a loving groom, this man dumped his load as quickly as possible on the couch. While she scrambled for the afghan tossed over the back, he plopped down in a nearby chair and began to rub his knee.

Kirby took advantage of his distraction to steal a good look at him. One adjective came to mind immediately: shaggy. Two others followed: big and tall. Some kind of backwoods mountain man? she wondered. Puzzled, she took note of his full beard, sky blue irises and tawny, too-long hair. Though easy on the eyes, he had a desperado look that made her heart thump with new fear. She huddled under the afghan. "What are you going to do to me?"

"Do?" He frowned at her. "I'm not going to *do* anything."

Kirby didn't believe him. He'd broken into her cabin, after all. One look around should have been enough to reveal nothing here worth stealing. Yet he'd still come right on into her bedroom. "But you attacked me."

He snorted at that. "In self-defense."

Kirby bristled. "Well, what did you expect? You broke into my cabin and—"

"*Your* cabin?" He arched an eyebrow at her.

"Yes. It belongs to me . . . and my sister."

He shook his head. "Nice try. But I happen to know it belongs to Jason Lawrence, who loaned it to me two months ago—"

"You've been in this cabin that long?" she gasped in outrage, getting to her feet and wrapping the afghan around her, sari style. She waddled over to the chair and glared down at him.

"That's right," he told her. "All alone and praying for a surprise visit from a Muse." He laughed shortly at his little joke and gave her a once-over the likes of which she hadn't had since college. "I don't suppose your name is Clio, or Calliope, or—"

"My name is Kirby," she snapped, as irritated with him as with her brother-in-law's latest shenanigan. "And for your information, this place is not Jason's to loan. Now I suggest you get your stuff and get out of here before the roads become impassable."

"No way. Jason told me I could stay here for as long as I wanted. I'm not leaving."

"But he had no right."

"He had a key."

"Which he stole from his wife."

"Are you telling me that Madison Lawrence is your sister?" he interjected, standing to tower over her.

Kirby took a reflective step back. "Y-yes."

His eyes swept her. "I don't believe you."

"Why not?"

"Because you two don't look a bit alike."

"I know," she grumbled, used to the comparison by which she usually came up lacking. She pointed to a photograph hanging on the wall behind the hall tree. "Take a look at that."

Matt glanced to where she pointed, narrowed his eyes, then glanced back again. "So old Jason is your brother-in-law."

"That's right."

"You must be proud of him. The man is brilliant."

"He's lucky, that's all."

"Luck has nothing to do with his success. He has a head for business and an eye for raw talent."

Kirby laughed derisively. "You, I suppose?"

"I *am* one of his authors."

"Don't tell me, let me guess. You write Westerns."

"No."

She rubbed her chin and made a show of eyeing him from head to toe. "Hmm. Science fiction?"

He shook his head.

"I've got it! Pornography."

He bristled visibly. "For your information, I write mainstream—political intrigue, to be exact."

Kirby's jaw dropped. "You're kidding."

"Cross my heart," he told her, doing exactly that for emphasis.

"And Jason is your publisher?"

"That's right."

"But he doesn't publish hardcover except for..." Her eyes rounded. "Surely you're not... You can't be..." She gulped. "Don't tell me you're Matt Foxx."

He grinned, clearly pleased by her awe. "All right, I won't."

"But you are?"

"The one and only."

Kirby gaped at him in disbelief. *This* was Matt Foxx—the most widely read author of political thrillers since Tom Clancy? Surely not. The Matt Foxx who headlined so many of the supermarket tabloids was cleanshaven and quite attractive. This man could pass for a hobo.

"I don't believe you."

"But it's true." He dug into the back pocket of his tattered jeans and produced a wallet. From it he extracted a card, which he handed to her.

Kirby immediately recognized the logo of her brother-in-law's publishing firm, embossed in gold across the top. Below that was typed *Matt Foxx* and the ID number assigned to him by the security division. She caught her breath and handed the card back, her head spinning with this opportunity. Not in the least fond of Ross Elliot, the chauvinistic CIA agent around whom Matt's bestsellers revolved, Kirby had often fantasized about meeting—and ventilating to—his playboy creator.

"This is such a surprise, Mr. Foxx," she said, extending her hand. "I've read a couple of your books. They were very...um...*interesting*."

The answering twinkle in his eye told her he suspected she wasn't a fan. "Why, thanks, Kirby. I may call you that...?"

"I—I guess so."

"Good. And you must call me Matt," he said. "We're sharing a roof, after all."

"We are?" She barely heard him, most of her concentration on finding a way to tactfully verbalize her disgust for his main character . . . and him.

"Unless you were serious about sending me packing. Frankly I hope you weren't. I've got a temporary case of writer's block and I'm past deadline. I was counting on these four walls to provide me with some much-needed privacy and inspiration, but so far all I've done is climb them."

"Is that so?"

"Yes. Please let me stay. I promise I won't bother you." He strode over to the bunk beds, built years ago for Madison and Kirby when their mother ran away to live life in the fast lane. "I'll sleep here," he said, patting the thin mattress of the bottom bed. "And I'll move my word processor off the kitchen table and set it—" he scanned the living room "—on one of those."

"You can't type on a TV tray."

"But I don't want to tie up the kitchen table."

"We can eat in here by the fire," she offered absently, her mind still spinning with half-formed plans.

"That's a great idea. And while we're on the subject of eating . . . I picked up quite a few groceries yesterday. I'll be glad to share." He gave her a brilliant smile.

"I brought enough for an army myself," Kirby told him, momentarily dazzled by those even white teeth and his killer charm. No wonder women the world over swooned at his feet.

"Then we'll have plenty to eat. And since I chopped wood all morning, we'll have that fire, too."

"You chopped the wood on the front porch?"

"That's right, and I have the aching muscles to prove it."

He flexed his right arm, a move that stretched the fabric of his plaid flannel shirt and revealed biceps worth writing home about. Lost in feminine appreciation, Kirby made no reply.

"Why don't I get my things out of the bedroom right now so you can get dressed?" Matt said, moving toward the door with determined strides. "Then I'll help you unpack these boxes."

Without waiting for her response, he disappeared from view. Only then did Kirby realize what she'd done. At once her knees threatened to buckle. She groaned softly and sank into the chair recently vacated by her guest.

Had she actually agreed to let him stay? Matt Foxx, world-famous author, notorious jet-setter, *total stranger?*

Silently Kirby scolded herself for losing control of the situation—something she rarely did. She considered her options and decided there were two: throw him out or let him stay. If she threw him out, she would undoubtedly embarrass Jason and further alienate her love-blind sister, who believed her husband could do no wrong. Kirby really didn't want to do that. As it was, she and Madison argued every time they got together these days.

And then there was Matt and the little matter of his deadline. How could she, an efficiency consultant, banish this obviously disorganized man without first showing him how much more productive his life could be with the help of a little self-discipline? Why, he might never finish this book or any others—which would not be such a tragedy, now that she thought about it.

Nonetheless, he needed her expertise, whether he knew it or not, and she couldn't in good conscience deny it or toss aside what could well be a chance to suggest a few changes to soften his macho main character. Could she really turn down such a marvelous opportunity?

"Absolutely," Kirby said, suddenly remembering her sister's recent accusation that she wasn't happy unless managing other people's lives. Had Madison been right, after all? Was Kirby as compulsive and bossy as her younger sister claimed? Was that why she was in such a quandary of indecision over Matt?

"Damn that Jason Lawrence," Kirby muttered in disgust. The man had no scruples—the reason for this unholy mess and her resulting confusion.

As for Matt Foxx, if the scandal sheets were anything to go by, he and Jason had much in common. She'd be nothing less than a fool if she wasted her time and talents on a globe-trotter who reportedly used personal experience as a basis for the bedroom antics of his main character. Matt was undoubtedly as chauvinistic as that character—the kind of man who wouldn't take advice from a female on his books or his life. She was simply going to have to be assertive and make him leave. She had no other choice.

* * *

In the bedroom, Matt gave himself another mental pat on the back for his usual brilliance in handling a tricky situation, then tried to squash his suitcase shut. Filled to capacity and then some, it wouldn't close. He grumbled good-naturedly, tucked it under his arm and gave the double bed a long look of regret.

He was going to miss that bed. It was soft, warm and conducive to a good night's sleep. Built for two, it also had the potential to wreck a man's sleep—provided he had a willing woman curled up next to him.

Matt glanced speculatively toward the door to the living room. Would Kirby Lee Gibson consider sharing that big ol' bed? he wondered, a second later grinning at the crazy direction his thoughts had taken. From all indications, Kirby didn't even like him—quite a novelty these days.

And though she had agreed to let him stay in her cabin, he was pretty darned sure he could still find himself out on his ear if he didn't mind his manners. If that happened, he would have no excuse not to finish his book, which meant he would have to admit once and for all that he'd lost his touch.

Since Matt wasn't quite ready to do that, he hoped Kirby *had* been sent by the Muses to energize him. So what if he'd never worked with a partner before and didn't intend to start now? He was still damned grateful to those goddesses of inspiration, who must have taken note of his current creativity problems and decided to intercede. Kirby was going to be a definite stimulus. Why, he could actually feel his creative juices—well, some kind of juices—already beginning to flow.

With a grin and a last look around to see if he'd missed anything essential for survival, Matt said goodbye to that cozy room. He headed out into the living room, where Kirby now stabbed a poker at the smoldering logs in the fireplace.

"Here," he said, tossing his suitcase onto the top bunk and reaching for the ornate metal rod. "Let me show you how to get a fire going."

"I can manage," she tartly informed him.

He winced at her tone. Second thoughts already?

"I've been thinking," Kirby said then, as though reading his mind. "And I've decided it would be better for all concerned if you went to a motel—Jason's treat, of course. This whole mix-up is his fault."

"You're turning me out?" Matt asked, trying to ignore his rising panic that his lustful thoughts about Kirby had angered his benefactors, who now intended to take back their gracious gift.

"Yes. I planned this holiday very carefully. There's no room for you in my plans."

"But I'll keep to myself. You won't even notice I'm around."

"Of course I will, and you'll notice I'm around, too. You said you came up here to write. I'm bound to distract you."

Matt, who desperately hoped so, began to argue. "I've been here alone for two months and written a grand total of ten pages. I've got a bad case of cabin fever—a really bad case. I've procrastinated until I'm not even sure I can finish this book. I need you, Kirby."

"Me?" She looked doubtful, but intrigued—definitely intrigued.

Matt shrugged with calculated casualness and gave her a smile of apology. "Sorry, I guess I *am* asking a hell of a lot. Probably the last thing you want to do over the Christmas holidays is rescue a washed-up writer."

Kirby's brown eyes narrowed speculatively. "Rescue? As in help you write your book?"

"Why not?" he blurted, momentarily addled by her wholesome good looks. Her cheeks glowed with health. Her full lips begged to be kissed, as did her uptilted nose, lightly dusted in freckles. She was pretty with a capital *P,* and caught up in his appreciation of her, Matt barely had wits to add, "What I mean is, you could act as sounding board to a plot twist I've been playing with. Who better than someone who hates my books?"

"Oh, I don't hate them," Kirby said, blushing attractively. "I just don't care for their star." She chewed her bottom lip in obvious uncertainty. Matt wondered at her reluctance and the speculative gleam in her eye. It was almost as though she were caught up in some heavy inner struggle. Did that mean his Muse theory was all wet? That she actually had a reason for coming up here to spend Christmas alone?

"So you don't like Ross. Well, you're not alone. Now's your chance to ventilate and maybe even suggest some changes to smooth out his rough edges. You have a captive audience." Surely she couldn't resist such an offer.

But still she hesitated.

"What's wrong?" Matt finally asked. "Don't you trust me?"

"Frankly, no," Kirby answered, meeting his gaze head-on. "And why should I? We've just met, after all, and your reputation precedes you."

So that was it. Kirby Lee Gibson was one of the millions who read and believed the lies Jason manufactured to boost sales. That meant she thought Matt slept with anything in skirts and squandered his "millions" on booze. Though he usually welcomed the notoriety he believed so essential in preserving the secrecy of his alter ego, Dillon Mathias, Matt now felt moved to defend his honor.

"What can I say to convince you what a nice man I really am?" he asked, not for the first time amazed at the gullibility of the public. What would happen if they discovered that the jet-setting creator of Ross Elliot was also the never-interviewed, never-photographed creator of the Skeeter Skunk and Friends series? Matt sincerely believed both careers would go up in smoke, the reason he went along with the playboy image Jason had manufactured. Sometimes—like now—he grew weary of the charade, however, and of conniving women with smiles on their faces, time on their hands and bank accounts instead of hearts. "What if I told you I was an Eagle Scout when I was in my teens?"

"Were you?"

"No, but I once helped a little old lady cross the street."

"I'm sure she appreciated it."

"Actually she whacked me with her umbrella." He shrugged. "How was I supposed to know she was liberated?"

Kirby's eyes began to twinkle. Matt could see that she struggled not to smile...a good sign, to his way of thinking. "Anything else I should know?"

"Let's see.... I once risked my neck getting a cat out of a tree."

"And how did that turn out?"

"Damned thing scratched me." He pointed to his cheek, just under his eye. "There's still a scar here someplace."

Kirby joined him and bent down slightly, peering at his face. "Whose cat was it?"

"My little sister's."

"You have a sister?"

"Two of them, actually."

"Any brothers?"

"No."

"Are your parents living?"

"Yes, and both sets of grandparents."

Kirby straightened and gave him a half smile. "You're very lucky, you know. My grandmother—the one I knew, at least—is dead."

"I'm sorry."

"Me, too. I hope you visit yours often."

"Since Granny and Gramps live in San Bernardino and Nana and Paps live in Baton Rouge, I don't get to visit with them as often as I'd like to. I do call them every weekend, though.''

"Really?"

Matt nodded.

"That's nice," Kirby murmured. "Very nice." Unexpectedly she added, "I guess you can stay."

Matt arched an eyebrow in surprise at his easy victory.

"What made you change your mind?" he asked, just enough gun-shy of ulterior motives to be suspicious of Kirby's abrupt about-face. "The little old lady or the cat?"

"Neither. I figure that any man who can refer to his grandmother as 'Nana' without blushing can't be all bad." She smiled then, a full-blown smile that revealed two dimples. Matt groaned silently at the sight, at once wondering if it were Venus and not the Muses who'd taken a good look at his miserable life and decided to intervene. Kirby Lee Gibson was more than just pretty. She was long-nights, happy-days, forever-after gorgeous.

And sharing a roof with her might not be such a brilliant idea, after all. A susceptible bachelor such as he—burned-out, brain-dead, at the crossroads of the rest of his life—had no business spending time alone with such a charmer, much less carrying her panties around in his pocket. Thank God she didn't like him or have designs on the income vastly exaggerated by Jason to the press.

Or did she? Warily Matt eyed his hostess, wondering what had really changed her mind about letting him, a virtual stranger, stay in her cabin. Was it his plea for help? Or something altogether different?

Kirby had as good as admitted she'd read all about him. Had she somehow figured out that Matt Foxx was not nearly as macho as his main character, Love-Em-and-Leave-Em Elliot? Had she heard his heart hammer every time she smiled? Seen the flush on his face, the tremble of his hands? Did she now intend to take advantage of his addled state to charm him out of a fortune that only existed in the gossip columns?

There was a good chance, he realized, vividly remembering another time, another woman. He'd learned a valuable lesson then—a lesson he swore he'd never, ever forget.

So why did he know in his gut that Dillon Mathias Foxx, alias Dillon Mathias alias Matt Foxx, was in big trouble again?

Chapter Two

"Thanks. That's great. Really great." Matt barely managed a smile.

There was an awkward silence, during which he avoided further eye contact, his thoughts on his car, the snowy roads and escape. Was it too late to get the heck out of Dodge? he suddenly wondered.

"There is a catch, though."

He tensed at Kirby's choice of words. "And what's that?"

"You have to promise to listen to standard lecture number three—*Never Waste a Minute*." She smiled at his bewilderment. "I'm an efficiency expert for Time Is Money, Inc. I'd be less than honest if I didn't admit that I think you could well be the biggest challenge of my career."

Though vastly relieved by this revelation of her real motives, Matt bristled. "I resent that. We just met, for pete's sake. How could you possibly call me inefficient?"

Kirby tossed her almost-dry curls over her shoulder and gave him a censorious look. "I seem to recall your saying you'd been up here two whole months and written next to nothing. If that isn't inefficient, I don't know what is."

She had a point, Matt realized. But his condition was only temporary. He'd be his usual, highly productive self in no time—whether or not she stayed, lectured or otherwise inspired him.

"And that's the real reason why you're letting me stay?" he asked just to make sure his fictional wealth and fun-loving image had nothing whatsoever to do with anything. "Because I present some kind of challenge to you?"

Kirby nodded solemnly.

"Hmm." He eyed her in silence for a moment, mentally acknowledging that she wasn't the only person in the cabin who loved challenges. He loved them, too—especially challenges as curvaceous as this lovely young woman with nothing but business on her mind. What a refreshing change, and since Matt had something besides business on his, being the object of Kirby's energies and undivided attention didn't sound so very bad. Neither did a lecture, he decided, provided they were horizontal when she delivered it.

"So... are you willing?"

Willing? Try eager... to get horizontal with her, anyway. He managed a casual shrug. "I think it's a total waste of time, but what the hey.... If you want to talk, I'll listen."

"Good. You won't regret it. Now, are you finished in the bedroom? I want to get out of these, um—" Kirby glanced down at the afghan enshrouding her and laughed softly "—designer duds and into something more my style."

"I'm finished," Matt replied. "Are you hungry? I could throw together some supper while you change."

"Oh, would you? I'm starved. I was on the road most of the day and didn't take time for more than a salad for lunch."

"You're from Wyoming?"

"Yes. Cheyenne, to be exact. What about you?"

"Seattle, Washington. How was the highway today?"

"Bad and getting worse," Kirby told him. "I really had to keep my wits about me. No looking at the scenery."

"Then I'll bet you're as tired as you are hungry."

"Hungrier, by far."

Matt laughed. "Is that my cue to exit to the kitchen?"

"Uh-huh, and thank you for volunteering chef duties tonight. I'll do the washing up." Clutching the front hem of her afghan to keep from tripping on it, she made her way to the bedroom with shuffling steps. The back of it trailed behind her, much like the train of a wedding gown, a simile that surprised Matt, who seldom had marriage or anything remotely connected to it on his mind.

"W-what sounds good to you?" he stammered, disturbed by his runaway thoughts.

"Anything," Kirby responded as she reached the door and disappeared through it.

Since Matt had only one specialty—breakfast—her choice suited him fine. He headed to the kitchen with determined strides. Twenty minutes passed before Kirby joined him there. The moment she did, he remembered her panties, still stashed in his pocket. Had she missed them? he wondered. Gone without?

Get a grip! he immediately scolded himself even as his libido went berserk... again. Bemused, Matt actually began to wonder at the intensity of his desire for Kirby, who'd entered his life mere minutes ago. Sure she was attractive, but he'd met many attractive females in his thirty-seven years and almost always managed to keep his cool, not to mention his distance.

Never had he felt so... out of control, so... determined to be one with a woman. It was almost as though their meeting had been destined. As though he'd waited all his life for Kirby and, now that she was here, couldn't wait to begin their eternity together....

Eternity? Matt choked back an astonished laugh and admonished himself for his foolishness. Sure, she was different from the other women he'd met, but that was no reason to lose his head.

"Something smells wonderful," Kirby murmured, walking to stand next to him at the massive electric stove, the only concession to modern times Matt had found in this old cabin besides a hot-water heater, a refrigerator and an antiquated washing machine. She eyed the platter of fried ham, sniffed suspiciously at the skillet of bubbling gravy and turned to him. "What else are we having?"

"Scrambled eggs, biscuits and coffee," Matt said, taking a step back so that the all-woman, honeysuckle scent of her wouldn't distract him from the task at hand.

"Breakfast for dinner?"

"Don't tell me you've never done that?"

"Can't say that I have." She sounded doubtful about doing it now. "What can I do to help?"

"You can take a seat right over there," Matt replied, pointing to the kitchen table, several safe feet away. "I never could do anything with someone watching over my shoulder."

"I understand perfectly." She walked to the table, pulled out one of the ladder-back chairs and sat. Silence reigned for a moment, then she said, "Tell me more about your family."

"What do you want to know?" he asked, outwardly cool, inwardly near boiling point. A quick glance at Kirby revealed that she wore crimson stretch pants and an oversize, multicolor ski sweater.

And he'd thought long johns were sexy.

"Tell me about your nana," Kirby said. She crossed her legs at the knee and began to swing her sock-covered foot. "That's what I called my grandmother, too, by the way."

Nana. At the mention of his relative's pet name, Matt suddenly remembered a conversation he'd had with that dear lady just days ago. Obviously picking up on the restlessness that haunted him lately, she'd suggested that an occasional date might relieve his boredom. Matt had given her his standard I'm-not-interested-in-romance answer, then suffered through a fifteen-minute discourse on old age, finding the right woman and settling down.

That, no doubt, was the reason for these nuptial notions now. Nana had somehow planted a seed, which these two lonely months had nurtured into a thriving weed.

Well, there was no room for weeds among the hybrid ideas blooming in Matt's bachelor brain. And for that reason he yanked this particular one out by its roots. All he wanted from Kirby was a diversion. If things got hot and heavy—fantastic. If they didn't, he'd live. He could take or leave Kirby Gibson and certainly didn't need her or any woman to help him "settle down."

"Nana's real name is Marie Renee Bishop. She's my mother's mother and was born in New Orleans of Spanish and French parents. She speaks three languages, paints exquisite watercolor portraits and is remarkably active for her seventy-one years."

"She sounds special."

"She is." Matt cracked four eggs into a bowl and whipped them to frothy gold with a fork. "Now tell me about your nana."

"Her real name was Susannah Gibson. She was a seamstress most of her life, but was only working now and then by the time I met her because of a vision problem."

Matt poured the eggs onto the heated griddle and began to stir them with a spatula. "And when was that?"

"Fifteen years ago last month. I was thirteen—Madison was eight."

Though extremely curious as to why Kirby waited until she was a teenager to meet her grandmother for the first time, Matt didn't pursue it. Instead, he scraped the done-to-a-turn eggs into a bowl, which he set on the warm center of the stove. "You and your sister have very unusual names. How'd your mom come up with them?"

She hesitated for a second, twisting a strand of curly golden hair around one finger. "They're our fathers' last names."

Matt digested that in silence. "So you two are half sisters."

"That's right."

"No wonder you don't look alike," he commented as he retrieved golden-browned biscuits from the oven and set them beside the eggs. "You must each have inherited your looks from your fathers."

"I really couldn't say," Kirby commented, getting to her feet. Once again she joined him at the stove, her eyes on the food. "Are you almost finished? I'm not sure I can wait another minute."

Though bursting with curiosity, Matt let her change the subject. "I'm *all* finished, actually." He handed her a plate from the cupboard. "Help yourself. Coffee's over there. I'll put the jelly, butter, salt and pepper on a tray and take them to the living room."

"Don't do it on my account. Jelly is full of sugar, butter is loaded with fat and cholesterol, salt is bad for your blood pressure," Kirby said as she took her plate and put a dainty helping of eggs and a biscuit on it.

"And you only eat what's good for you?" Matt asked incredulously, following suit but with much bigger portions.

"That's right."

"Does that mean no hot-fudge sundaes, greasy hamburgers or peanuts?"

"Not if there are other choices."

"How boring," he commented, horrified.

"I call it sensible."

Matt grimaced, then took up the spoon and deliberately ladled a generous portion of gravy over the ham, eggs and biscuits heaped on his plate. "Are you this *sensible* about everything you do?"

"I try to be." She set her food on the counter and pointed to the pot of coffee sitting on a back burner of the stove. "Decaffeinated?"

He shook his head.

Kirby reached into the cupboard for a glass, which she filled with tap water.

Matt chuckled.

"What's so funny?" she demanded, glaring at him.

"You are," he replied. "I'll bet you don't have a spontaneous bone in your body."

"That's a hateful thing to say."

"But true. You're compulsive, and I can prove it. Have you ever left your umbrella at home when it was cloudy?"

"Now, why would I do that?"

"So you could walk in the rain."

Kirby wrinkled her nose. "I might catch cold or ruin my clothes. Dry cleaning costs a fortune these days, you know." Plate in one hand, glass in the other, she whirled and headed for the living room.

Matt poured himself a cup of hot, caffeine-loaded coffee and took a sip of it. He sighed his satisfaction with life's simple pleasures, then followed Kirby.

"Have you ever set the alarm so you could get up at 4:00 a.m. to watch a sci-fi movie on TV before leaving for work?" he asked once he'd sat beside her on the couch.

Kirby gave him a hard look. "I hate science fiction," she replied around a mouthful of unbuttered, unjellied biscuit. "And even if I didn't, I wouldn't do that. Too much television is bad for your eyes. Any more questions?"

"Just one. Have you ever gone out with a man because he turned you on and *not* because he had a steady job, a nice personality or good manners?"

Her jaw dropped. "Don't be ridiculous."

"You've never met a man who'd turned you on?"

"I'd never waste my time dating someone I wouldn't marry. What if I pulled the same stunt my sister pulled and fell in love?"

"I rest my case."

Kirby stared at him for a long moment, vastly irritated by his questions and his conclusion. "Just because I eat right, take precautions against bad weather, hate TV and choose my dates carefully is no reason to call me compulsive."

"Overdoing those things is," he retorted. "Some-day you're going to wake up and discover you've been so busy living right that you never lived." With that, Matt stuffed the last bite of his gravy-coated meal into his mouth.

At once Kirby's own mouth watered with the desire to taste that yummy-looking gravy. As disturbed by the unexpected craving as by his words—an echo of Madison's mere days before—she got to her feet to take her empty plate to the kitchen. Once there she filled the sink with hot water, then added a generous squirt of liquid detergent and her dirty dishes.

After snatching up a cloth, Kirby washed her plate with agitated swipes. Is he right? she wondered. Am I compulsive? Being called that twice in a week was a bit much, especially since the label had come from someone who knew her—Madison—and someone who didn't—Matt.

Admittedly she was a creature of habit—one of the reasons she excelled at her profession. When Kirby discovered the best way to do something, she did it that way from then on. That just made sense, and people such as Madison, who never thought past the end of her nose, or Matt, who had to be banished to the wilds of Wyoming before he could finish a book, really got on her nerves.

She got on their nerves, too, as a rule. Clearly Matt would be no exception. Their last conversation had revealed that they were opposites. That meant they would be at each other's throat in no time—exactly as she and Madison always were. Kirby must have been insane to tell him he could stay, much less to think she could change him.

After rinsing her plate, fork and glass, Kirby attacked the stove top with the washcloth. In a skillet on the front burner was the gravy, rich and hot. Kirby glanced quickly toward the living room, wiped her free hand dry on her slacks and reached for one of the leftover biscuits, which she broke apart. In one guilty motion, she dipped a bite-sized bit into the gravy and popped it into her mouth.

"Aha!"

Kirby gasped at the sound of Matt's voice from the doorway and sucked the forbidden morsel down her throat, nearly choking to death in the process.

"Are you okay?" Matt asked, striding up as though he had every intention of performing the Heimlich maneuver. Kirby threw up her hand, palm outward, to hold him at bay.

"Just dandy," she snapped between coughs. She snatched a glass from the cabinet and filled it with water, then took a swallow to cool her burning throat.

She wished she could cool her flaming cheeks that easily. Kirby felt incredibly foolish—like the child caught dipping into the proverbial candy jar. Lips pursed together in annoyance, she turned her back on her annoying guest and tossed the dishcloth into the sink.

"It was just a joke, for pete's sake," Matt said. "Nothing to get angry about."

"I'm not angry... at least not at you."

"At who, then? Yourself? Lighten up, Kirby. There's no sin in sneaking a bite of gravy."

Kirby whirled to face him then. "There is if you're watching your weight."

"Sometimes one bite is enough to satisfy the craving."

"And what if it's not?"

"You take one more."

"Which is exactly what I'm trying to avoid."

"But you're tiny."

"Only because I don't sneak bites of gravy." Kirby heaved a sigh of exasperation. "Oh, Matt. We're so very different."

He grinned. "Yeah . . . in all the right places."

He's flirting! "I—I meant our personalities," Kirby stammered, rattled that he would even bother. If Matt was anything like his creation, Ross Elliot, she wasn't remotely his type. "We . . . I . . ." Kirby took a calming breath and told herself Matt was teasing, not flirting. "I'm structured and organized. You're freestyle and have no self-discipline, which is why you can't finish your stupid book."

"Well, if I don't have any self-discipline, it's because you got more than your fair share."

Resisting the urge to wring his handsome neck, Kirby turned her back on him and tackled the rest of the dirty dishes.

"This isn't going to work, you know," she said after a weighty silence.

"What isn't?" Matt asked, again from the doorway. He strode to the sink and submerged the plate, mug and fork he'd apparently just retrieved from the living room.

"Our cohabitation," she told him.

Matt said nothing, and when Kirby turned to see why, she found herself eye to chin with him, a highly disconcerting proximity...even if he was just teasing. Her heart skipped a beat. "I should never have agreed to let you stay, and if you had any tact at all you'd do the noble thing and leave tonight. You could spend Christmas with those grandparents you love. I'm sure *they'd* be thrilled to have you around for the holidays."

"But what would you do all alone up here?"

"Exactly what I planned to do in the first place," she said. "Enjoy the peace, quiet and time off. And as soon as I leave, you can come back to finish your book."

"How do you expect me to finish it if you don't share your time-management secrets with me?"

Dubious of his sincerity, Kirby perused Matt's guileless expression. He met her gaze without once blinking those thickly-lashed eyes of his or sharing that gorgeous smile. "Let me get this straight.... You're admitting you're disorganized?"

"Let's just say that I believe you're a gift from the gods. The sooner you work your magic, the better. Why, we could start tonight...."

"You mean you want to hear my lecture *now?*"

He frowned. "Your...? Oh, uh...sure. Why not? It's early yet. Why not deliver standard lecture number—was it two?"

"Three," she supplied, now seriously doubting his motives for hanging around. Was the "help" he needed for his book really nothing but more research on the steamy seductions at which his favorite character excelled? Or was he simply so bored with himself that any diversion would do? Probably the latter, Kirby decided. It was green-eyed, redheaded Madison who attracted rogues such as Matt, not her dishwater blond older sister.

"Three, then," he said. "What do you say? Are you going to save a drowning man or not?"

Kirby hesitated, completely at a loss. "If I do, it'll be too late for you to leave tonight."

"So I'll leave first thing tomorrow...if you still want me to."

She winced at his reply, which did not clarify his motives one whit. "Of course I'll want you to."

Matt shrugged. "Then I'll go." That said, he left the room.

With growing unease, Kirby finished washing up. Minutes later she joined Matt in the living room, where he worked building up the fire. He flashed that sexy smile of his the moment she walked in the room. Kirby noticed that he'd turned off the ceiling light, leaving the flickering flames as sole illumination. Shadows waltzed over the walls to cluster in the corners of the room. Outside, the wind howled—chilly wind that had nothing whatsoever to do with the goose bumps tickling Kirby's skin.

"Where do you want to do this?" Matt asked.

"Do what?" she asked, heart in her throat.

"Give your lecture, of course." His frown asked if she'd lost her mind.

"Oh." Kirby laughed nervously and gave herself a mental kick in the backside. What was she so worried about? The odds against Matt's wanting to seduce a "compulsive" efficiency expert with freckles were surely phenomenal. And besides, she knew how to protect herself if he got amorous. Another kick to the knee would probably do him in. "Since I can't really see me standing at the front of the room and making a formal delivery, why don't we just sit on the couch?"

"Would you mind if we were closer to the fire, like on the rug, here?"

She tensed, at once suspicious again. "Why?"

"I've been cold ever since I came in this evening."

"Oh." Kirby swallowed hard. "You aren't getting sick, are you?"

"I hope not. I thought cabin fever was bad enough." He grinned when she rolled her eyes, then grew serious. "Actually I spent most of the day outside and got a little damp, that's all."

"What you need is a hot shower."

"Later. Now I want to hear what you have to say." He brushed off his hands and sat on the rug, the stone hearth to his left.

After a fractional hesitation, Kirby sat cross-legged, facing him. "Have you ever had any kind of efficiency training?"

"What do you think?" he asked with a chuckle, easing forward until their knees touched.

"I think I'll begin at the beginning." And she did, taking a full half hour to share simple, time-tested principles of productivity. By the time she finished talking, Matt had stretched out on his side, propping his elbow on the floor and his head in his hand. His body, long and oh-so-male, was mere inches away, and more than once Kirby's attention strayed from the here and now to a never-never land where women did irresponsible things such as lie down next to total strangers and make the most of a winter night, a cozy fire and a secluded cabin. Horrified at that traitorous thought, she halted her lecture rather abruptly. "That's it. Any questions?"

"No, but I have a confession to make."

"You snoozed through half my explanation?"

He sat up, obviously offended, then leaned forward till they were eye-to-eye. "I heard every word. I now know how important it is to plan my workday, avoid distractions, sidestep procrastination, set reasonable goals, take regular breaks and reward myself for a job well done."

"You did listen!"

He nodded. "I listened, and though you have a lot of good ideas, I have to admit I don't believe they apply to writing."

"And why is that?" she demanded, as flustered by his comment as by his face, so kissably close. Kirby, who'd once kissed a date with a beard and hated it, thanked her lucky stars for Matt's whiskers. They were all that kept her from satisfying a sudden urge to find out if his kisses were as potent as Ross Elliot's always were.

"We're artists. We create when we burn with an idea, which is not necessarily when the clock strikes nine, ten or whatever, Monday through Friday." He reached out to Kirby and gently brushed back a lock of hair that had fallen over one eye. Her heart slammed into her rib cage.

At once highly aware of the sorts of differences Matt had mentioned earlier, Kirby scrambled to her feet to look down at him. "It's all a matter of cueing yourself—a matter of ritual and routine."

"It'll never work."

"Not if you don't try it."

"But I wouldn't know how to begin setting up a daily schedule."

"I'll help you."

"Tomorrow?"

She hesitated. "I guess we could do that before you leave."

"Leave? You're actually going to schedule my life and then walk out of it? What if I have questions? What if things don't work out as planned?"

Kirby huffed her exasperation and deliberately kept her gaze above his full lips so she could think straight. "I've only promised to help you get set up. I'm not taking you to raise. If things don't work out, you won't be one bit worse off than you are now."

"And if you donate a few days of your holiday to my cause, you won't be, either. All I'm asking is your undivided attention until I get on the right track. I'll do anything you say. Imagine the thrill of converting me, the 'biggest challenge of your career,' into a writer who can be creative on demand."

Kirby could well imagine being thrilled by Matt Foxx, but the vision in her usually level head had little to do with his writing. Baffled by this unexpected, unwanted physical attraction, she acknowledged that changing the man would be no bigger a challenge than resisting him. Thank goodness for that awful beard.

"Well . . . what do you say?"

"I say . . ." she gulped. "I say 'why not?' And if *that* isn't spontaneous, I don't know what is."

Matt laughed aloud at Kirby's words, a wonderful sound that shimmied down her spine and told her she'd probably just made the worst decision of her life. "You know, we both might learn from this encounter."

"Somehow I doubt it," Kirby said. She glanced at her watch. "I'm beat. You've got thirty minutes in the bathroom before I run you out."

"Yes, ma'am," he said, leaping to his feet. Matt snatched a gray sweatsuit and a travel kit from his overflowing suitcase, then headed for the bathroom without further ado.

Kirby sank to the rug and stared into the fire, only to get up again when Matt suddenly yelled for help. Reluctantly she joined him outside the bedroom, where he stood, tugging on the bathroom door she had locked from the inside not so long ago. Kirby quickly unlocked the door by inserting a hairpin into the hole in the doorknob. Moments later she walked back to the living room, shaking her head slowly in wonder.

So much for holidays spent in blessed solitude. Not that she'd really wanted to pass this one that way. She hadn't, and had only come to her nana's old home to prove Madison's decision to spend Christmas with Jason's family did not matter—or hurt—one bit.

It did, of course. Kirby had mothered Madison for too many years not to feel rejected by that decision. And she sincerely hoped a dread of spending the holiday by herself was the secret reason she'd let Matt stay and not some misguided passion for him. Heaven knows the challenge of organizing his life really had little to do with it, no matter how many times she told herself it did. Matt was a lost cause, and in her heart of hearts, she still knew she'd be crazy to waste time on him.

But what if her attraction to him *was* the culprit? What if her love-starved hormones—like her sister's—had suddenly rebelled after years of good behavior? What then?

I'll just have to be careful, Kirby told herself. Keep my distance, mind my p's and q's, stick to business.

She could surely do that. She'd undergone years of training, after all, and was a professional. What were a few days and nights spent with a client?

Nights?

Thank God for the beard.

"I'm finished and with minutes to spare."

Kirby got to her feet without looking Matt's way and dusted off her pants. A glance at the bunk bed in the corner of the living room confirmed that she would need to round up sheets and blankets before her guest could sleep. She turned to him, prepared to point out the linen closet.

"You'll find extra sheets and—" Words suddenly failed Kirby. Her knees turned to putty. She felt the blood drain from her cheeks.

"What is it?" Matt demanded, narrowing his gaze. "What's wrong?"

"You shaved."

He rubbed his freshly shaved, temptingly touchable jawline. "Yeah. Damned thing had started to itch." He frowned. "You don't like it?"

Kirby gulped. "Extra sheets and blankets are in the closet over there. I'm sure there are some to fit the bunk."

He glanced that way and back again. "Thanks. About the beard—"

"You look fine."

"You really think so?"

"Well . . . you could use a haircut."

"Yeah, I know. Got any scissors?"

Kirby's eyes widened. "You cut your own hair?"

"No. I thought you might cut it for me."

"Are you out of your mind? I'm no barber."

"Maybe not," he retorted. "But I'm willing to lay odds that you've cut a head of hair before."

"And what makes you say that?"

"The price of a haircut these days. A sensible young woman such as you has surely rebelled."

Kirby, who *had* rebelled and, as a result, given many a haircut in college, nonetheless shook her head. The thought of putting her hands in this mane of his made her head spin. "I'm not cutting your hair, and that's final. Now, I'm really very tired, so if you'll excuse me, I'll . . ."

"But we haven't changed *your* linens yet."

We? Didn't the poor man know the dangers of making beds with sex maniacs? His virtue now hung in the balance.

On that thought, Kirby's heart stopped, then kicked into overdrive.

If anyone's virtue was at stake, it was hers. And a man of the world such as Mr. Cleanshaven Foxx undoubtedly knew it.

Chapter Three

"I can manage alone," Kirby told him, walking quickly over to the closet and flinging the door open. She stepped inside, and from the ample supply of cotton sheets stacked on a shelf there, extracted both a fitted and flat one, sized for the bunk bed, and matching pillowcases. She turned, intending to toss them the few feet to Matt, but found him at her elbow instead. "T-these should work," she stammered, disconcerted by his proximity. She shoved the linens at his midsection.

"Thanks."

"How many blankets do you need?" Kirby held her breath to keep from inhaling too deeply the woodsy, all-man scent of his after-shave, which had permeated the tiny area. She deliberately kept her gaze below his chin, but above the rounded neck of the gray sweatshirt he wore.

"Just one, and I may not need it. I'm very hot natured."

Pretty darned sure he was hot-*blooded*, as well, Kirby dragged her attention back to the closet. She selected a dark blue thermal blanket she'd purchased for her sweet grandmother just last winter and handed it to him.

"There. You're all fixed up. Get busy."

For one second Kirby feared Matt was going to insist on helping her first. He certainly hesitated as though he might, but then he shrugged and pivoted to walk over to the narrow bunk. He set the bedclothes on the upper berth and began to strip the lower.

Kirby quickly grabbed another set of sheets—these to fit her own double bed—and four blankets, each of which she would need since she was as cold natured as Matt claimed to be the contrary. Stepping back, she kicked the closet door shut.

Though Kirby could see nothing around her unwieldy bundle, she could hear Matt off to her right, muttering as he struggled to put the fitted sheet on the mattress. Kirby wasn't at all surprised that he seemed to be having a difficult time of it. The head and one whole side of the beds were attached to the wall, and he was just tall enough to have to stand awkwardly stooped under the top bunk while he worked on the bottom one.

Kirby made her way gingerly into the bedroom, plotting her course with her toe. There she dumped her load. In seconds she stripped the bed and had almost finished remaking it when a loud thump and an even louder curse emanated from the living room.

Dropping the pillow she held, Kirby dashed next door just in time to see Matt give one of his a swift kick, which sent it flying halfway across the living room. He flushed when he realized he had an audience.

"I bumped my head," Matt mumbled by way of explanation, retrieving the pillow. After fluffing it, he frowned at the half-made bunk. "Good thing I was never in the military. I couldn't have passed inspection."

Kirby's gaze followed his down to the mattress, three corners of which were smoothly encased in a pastel blue sheet. The fourth corner stood bare, and judging from the scant amount of sheet left to stretch over and cover it, might be that way this time next year. Biting back a laugh—he *would* save the inside and hardest corner for last—Kirby joined him.

"You're going about this all wrong," she scolded. "You do the corners next to the wall first. Like this..."

In a split second she undid the handiwork of long minutes and stripped the mattress again. While Matt watched in silence, she then ducked under the top bunk, leaned over the bed and got to work.

Halfway through her task, Kirby sneaked a peek to see if Matt were properly impressed by her expertise. To her dismay, she found his gaze not on the mattress, but on her tush, stuck up in the air and most likely wiggling provocatively with every move she made.

And she'd wondered if he were hot-blooded.

Vastly irritated both with him and herself, Kirby made short work of slipping the sheet over the fourth and final corner. "There," she said, straightening. "See how easy that was? Now you're on your own. I have mine to do."

"I'll be glad to help," Matt offered again. "You did the same for me, after all...."

"No, thanks," Kirby said, knowing better than to share so intimate a task with him. Two long strides carried her back to the safety of her bedroom, two more took her to her bed, across which she fell face-down with a soft "ooph!"

Clearly she needed a brushup course on the complexities of the male libido—specifically on how not to excite it.

Brushup course? Kirby rolled on her back and laughed softly at herself. She didn't need a brushup. She needed a full-fledged, beginning-to-end, crash course. And no wonder. Though twenty-eight years old, Kirby had never shared a roof with a man for more than a week, and that particular one had spent most of his time in her mother's bedroom... with her mother.

Wrinkling her nose at the unpleasant memory, Kirby got to her feet and finished stuffing her pillows into their cases. Then she bundled up the discarded linens and headed to the kitchen, where her nana's old washing machine was located.

Kirby didn't speak to Matt as she darted through the living room, or even glance in the direction of his bunk. To her relief, he didn't say anything, either. When she burst into the kitchen, she found out why:

he wasn't in the living room. He was in the kitchen—standing in front of the open refrigerator.

"Just put those with that other stuff there on the floor," he told Kirby, waving his hand toward the washer. "I'll do them one of these days."

Kirby eyed the knee-high pile of what looked to be several weeks' worth of dirty laundry. "And what day might that be?"

Matt shrugged. "The day I run out of clean clothes." He peered into the refrigerator again. "Are you in the mood for a midnight snack? We have bologna, salami, two kinds of cheese...."

"Midnight snack?" Kirby couldn't believe her ears. "It's only nine-thirty and we just ate, for pete's sake."

"Maybe so, but I'm hungry again."

"No, you're not," Kirby told him, unceremoniously dumping her load. "You're bored. But not for long. I have plans for you, buster. Starting tomorrow."

The moment she said the words, she regretted them. Grinning, Matt gave her a lazy but thorough perusal that seemed to indicate he had plans for her, too—and why wait until tomorrow?

He slammed the refrigerator door shut. "I'm glad. Something tells me you're just what I need, Kirby Lee Gibson."

"Maybe you'd better reserve judgment," she warned. "Some of my clients have compared me to Captain Bligh." With her back ramrod straight, Kirby exited the kitchen and marched right on through the living room, not stopping until she reached her bedroom. She turned then to look at Matt, who had followed as far as the couch. "Do you need to get in the bathroom before I *lock* my door?"

That should discourage him.

Matt shook his head slowly from side to side. Kirby could have sworn he struggled not to smile.

"Then I'll say good night," she said quite coolly to hide her embarrassment. Obviously, sneaking into her room hadn't even crossed his mind. She had simply let her imagination run away with her. How humiliating.

And how...disappointing? Surely not.

Flustered by her wayward thoughts, Kirby stepped on into her bedroom and quickly shut the door but not before she heard Matt's soft "sleep tight."

Unfortunately Kirby didn't sleep "tight" or any other way. Instead, she lay in the antique iron bed, wide-eyed and wide-awake, listening to the sounds both inside and outside the hundred-year-old cabin.

Since she was fairly used to the wail of the winter wind, it was the noises that filtered into her bedroom from the living room, via the fireplace connecting them, that bothered her most.

Kirby heard every creak of Matt's bed, every rustle of his bedclothes, every soft, sexy sigh that seemed to come straight from his dreams. Were those dreams X-rated, she wondered?

Was she a star of them?

"Oh for...!" Kirby sat up and plumped her feather pillow with her fists, ventilating some of her frustration with herself. It wasn't as though she'd never been around a handsome, virile man before. She had. Dozens of them. Why, she'd even dated a few....

A *very* few. As a rule Kirby attracted men more interested in world affairs, their jobs or the stock market than in the opposite sex. According to Madison, Kirby had only herself to blame for that sad state of affairs because she ran like a scared rabbit every time any other kind of man showed the least bit of interest in her.

Kirby had always denied that accusation, but now she wondered. God knows she would certainly have run away this time if she could. But she couldn't. This cabin was hers, not Matt's. If anyone should leave the premises, it was he.

And why he now snored softly in the other room, she couldn't imagine or explain. She could begin formulating a daily schedule for him, though—one that would turn his life around so she could send him on his way in good conscience and as quickly as possible.

That acknowledged, Kirby abandoned her efforts to count sheep and turned her thoughts to something more worthwhile—time management.

Early Saturday morning, Kirby slipped out of bed and into the bathroom, where she made short work of her toilette. Shivering in the chilly air—the fire had long since died—she dressed in thick socks, faded jeans and a bulky red sweater, then opened the door to the living room.

She flicked on the overhead light and glanced toward the bunk bed to find that Matt still slept. Hoping he'd wake on his own, Kirby made as much noise as possible tossing logs into the grate and setting fire to them. She had much better luck this time than last night and was rewarded for her efforts by golden flames and blessed warmth.

But her luck ran out there, for Matt slept through everything.

Undaunted, Kirby next unpacked her boxes. She put everything neatly away, including the groceries and some books and magazines she'd been saving for free time.

Still Matt slept on.

Kirby glanced at her watch and realized she had no choice but to wake him so they could get on with his first day of disciplined living. Nervously gnawing her lower lip—she'd never woken a man before—Kirby approached the bed.

Matt lay on his side, his face to the wall, one arm free of the sheet that covered the rest of his body, his breathing slow and steady. Kirby noted that he more than filled the bunk both length- and width-wise, and guessed that might be the reason he'd tossed and turned most of the night.

Too bad she had to wake him now that he slept so blissfully, but her watch said it was after seven. According to her schedule, he'd overslept ten minutes already.

Kirby gingerly punched his bare shoulder with her fingertips. "Matt. Wake up."

He did not respond.

Bolder now of necessity, she put both hands to his muscled arm and shook him. "Matt!"

"Wha . . . ?" he mumbled, shaking off her touch.

"Wake up. It's time for your exercises."

Dead silence followed that statement, then Matt rolled over, clearly shocked to wide-eyed wakefulness. "My *what?*"

"Exercises—the first agenda item on the highly productive—" she hoped! "—daily schedule I've customized for you."

He squinted at his wristwatch and then at her in obvious disbelief. "You've got to be kidding."

"I never kid," Kirby replied, stepping back so he could get out of the bed. But he didn't get out. He rolled back over and covered his head with one of his pillows.

Kirby huffed her outrage. "Matt Foxx, you get out of that bed this minute!"

"Only a fitness fanatic would get up at this hour on a *Saturday* to exercise," he responded, his muffled words barely audible.

"I'll have you know I've been doing it for years," Kirby snapped, vastly irritated.

"I rest my case," Matt said, burrowing farther into the mattress.

"You do that a lot, don't you?"

"Only since you holed up in my cabin."

"It's *my* cabin!" Vastly irritated, Kirby yanked his pillow off the bed and let it drop to the floor. Then she put her sock-encased foot to the sheet draped over his backside to give him a not-so-gentle nudge. With a growl, Matt lifted his head just enough to give her a go-to-hell look over his shoulder.

"I am not a fitness fanatic," Kirby said now that she had his attention again. "I simply realize the value of exercise to overall well-being. I might add that a little exercise would do wonders for those love handles of yours, too."

"Love handles!" Matt exclaimed, clearly incensed. He sat bolt upright in the bed—or tried to. The top bunk successfully prevented that, but did not stop him from pushing the sheet off his broad, bare chest down to his equally bare waist, which he slapped with both hands. "Not an ounce of fat here. Not an ounce."

"It's a wonder, with the amount of food you eat," Kirby chided, carefully keeping her gaze level with his.

"Can I help it if I have a big appetite?" Matt lay back and locked his hands behind his head, his expression quite smug. "You can see it hasn't hurt me."

"Maybe not yet," she retorted. "But one of these days, it will catch up to you. That's why a good exercise program is so important. And that's why I decided you should begin each and every day with a light workout. Now, you either get with the program or get out. Take your pick."

Matt digested that in silence, his face growing redder with each passing moment. When he looked hot enough to explode, he sucked in a deep breath and closed his eyes.

After just enough time for someone to count silently to ten, he opened them again. "Okay. I'll get up... when *you* get out."

Kirby opened her mouth to remind him just who owned this cabin, but never uttered a word before a possible reason for his demand occurred to her. Since talking with a half-clothed—maybe even *unclothed*—man was one new experience too many to her way of thinking, she scurried back to her bedroom, slammed the door and didn't open it until Matt called out to her some ten minutes later.

"Request permission to visit the head, *Cap'n.*"

Kirby cautiously opened the door. After ascertaining that he was decently attired, she let him in. "Permission granted."

With a brisk nod, Matt swept past her and into the bathroom, shutting the door behind him. Smiling in spite of herself, Kirby walked back into the living room, where she retrieved her cassette player and a much-used audio tape from the table on which she had just placed them.

Just as she finished plugging in the player, Matt strolled into the room, his lower body respectably covered by a pair of jeans. As for his upper body... well, it wasn't covered or respectable.

It *was* awesome, however—smooth, muscled, tanned. No love handles on this specimen, no-siree... but she'd only said that to irritate him. Actually he appeared to be remarkably fit for a man with such a sedentary profession.

"I thought we could do the exercises over there," Kirby murmured, pointing to the only clear area of any size, the middle of the room. She spoke as calmly as possible, hoping Matt wouldn't see how his manly chest affected her topsy-turvy hormones.

Apparently her ruse worked. Matt merely shrugged. "If we must."

"Don't worry," Kirby told him. "We'll start out with a few easy stretches and work up to the harder stuff. You're going to do great. And when you finish, you'll *feel* great.''

''I never doubted it for a moment,'' Matt responded with sarcasm and just a little irritation. Absolutely the last thing he needed at seven-thirty on a Saturday morning was a Suzy Cheerleader who thought he should shape up—especially in light of all the money he'd spent furnishing his basement with workout equipment and the many hours he'd subsequently agonized down there.

Disgruntled, questioning his sanity for not leaving last night, he shuffled after her and stood waiting while she inserted a cassette into her tape player.

Suddenly loud rock music blared forth. Matt jumped in surprise.

''Ready?'' Kirby shouted over the din.

Still stunned, as much by the unexpected choice of music as by its volume, Matt barely managed a nod.

''All right!'' She faced him, placed her hands on her hips and scooted her feet apart slightly. ''Do exactly what I do,'' she instructed with a bright smile. Then she led him through a series of peppy warm-up moves so simple a toddler could ace them.

All that's missing are the pom-poms, Matt thought when she exclaimed, ''That's great! Keep it up!'' one time too many. He felt foolish...*incredibly* foolish.

Thank God my faithful fans can't see me.

''Now we're going to do a fitness routine I learned years ago,'' Kirby said. ''The first exercise is called a 'windmill.' Just watch me, and in no time you'll have the hang of it.''

She extended her arms out from her sides, bent over and touched the fingertips of her right hand to her left foot. After straightening to her original position, she repeated the move, but with her left hand to the right foot. Straightening again, she smiled encouragingly and asked, "Do you think you can do that?"

"Do I...?" At the end of his patience, Matt snarled his indignation and stomped over to the cassette player. He unplugged it with a yank of the cord and whirled on his hostess, whose eyes widened in alarm.

"You're damned right I can do that!" he told her. "Can *you* do *this?*" Bending over, he put his flattened palms to the floor and held that position for a painful count of ten.

"Well, I..."

"Can you?" he demanded, standing upright.

Kirby hesitated, then bent over and imitated his action. When she straightened, a count of ten later, her cheeks glowed crimson. "There. Satisfied?"

"Not by a long shot. Can you do this?" He dropped to the floor and did push-ups until his biceps, triceps and assorted other arm muscles screamed for mercy. Gasping for breath, but determined not to show it, he finally stopped and scrambled to his feet. "Your turn."

"I can only do modified push-ups," she said. "And I'm not sure how many."

"Do what you can."

She did and was as breathless as he when she finally collapsed onto her stomach with a groan. Without rolling over, she tipped her head back to meet his gaze. "What is this... mutiny already?"

Matt lowered himself to sit on the floor beside her. "Not quite. But you will have one if you insist on starting every day with 'a few light exercises.' I've had a universal workout unit in my basement for years, Kirby. I'm way past windmills on the living-room floor."

Kirby endured his accusing gaze for barely half a minute before she got to her feet and dusted off the cute little behind that had haunted his dreams the night before. "Well ex-*cuse* me. I was only trying to help."

She sashayed into the kitchen, leaving Matt alone and regretting he hadn't been just a little tactful. Cohabitation would definitely be a lot more fun if they were on speaking terms.

Cohabitation? With luck she might give him time to pack before she kicked him out.

Shaking his head in dismay, he rose and followed her, intent on making amends. "Why don't I put on a pot of coffee?"

"You know I don't drink coffee," Kirby replied, adding, "And neither should you. Why don't you try to wean yourself from that nasty stuff? Drink something that's good for you . . . like, say, milk or orange juice."

"Milk is for babies," Matt told her. "I'm thirty-seven years old. As for orange juice, well, I like it best at night with a bowl of popcorn."

"Good grief," Kirby replied. She sighed with what could have been mistaken for resignation—if Matt hadn't known better. "Drink your old coffee, then.

But first tell me what you want to eat with it. It's my turn to cook.''

"I don't want anything," Matt told her, busying himself filling the coffeepot with water and then measuring the rich-smelling grounds into the filter basket.

"You don't eat breakfast?" Kirby asked, clearly appalled.

Matt shook his head, set the pot on the stove and turned the flame up as high as it would go.

"Then it's no wonder you haven't been writing. You've denied your body the morning nutrition so essential for proper brain function, not to mention physical stamina."

"I've what—?"

"Never mind. You sit down right there." She pointed to the ladder-back chair she'd occupied the night before. "I'm going to cook up a breakfast that will really stick to your ribs."

"Please don't bother...." Matt protested rather weakly, his stomach already churning at the thought of facing food at this hour of the day. He'd never been one to eat earlier than noon—even before his arrival at the cabin when he'd begun to *sleep* until then.

"It's no bother," Kirby assured him. "And I promise you're going to be amazed by the increase in your productivity."

Against his better judgment, Matt did as requested and sat there in defiant silence until Kirby handed him a tray on which she had placed a bowl of hot oatmeal, a slice of dry toast and a glass of orange juice.

Only when he complained did she add a mug of hot black coffee.

A similarly laden tray in hand—orange juice instead of coffee, of course—Kirby then led the way to the living room, where she sat on one end of the couch and began to eat with gusto. Matt followed more slowly and only after he sneaked a heaping teaspoon of sugar and a tad of milk to make his oatmeal more palatable.

Unfortunately neither helped, and it was all Matt could do to choke down a bite.

"Now don't you feel better?" Kirby asked with nauseating cheerfulness when he set his tray aside.

"No."

"What a grump you are!" she exclaimed, heading to the kitchen with her tray.

"Not a grump," Matt retorted, snatching up his half-eaten breakfast and following. "A man who doesn't believe in living like a Spartan...or by a schedule."

Kirby slammed her tray down on the counter, then whirled on him. "I seem to recall that you *asked* me to help you. If you've changed your mind, just say so."

"I've changed my mind," he blurted.

"Fine. I'll help you pack." Never batting an eyelash, she left...probably to do just that.

Cursing under his breath, Matt ridded himself of his dishes and refilled his coffee cup. He took one fortifying swallow and then another, his eyes on the door through which Kirby had disappeared.

By the time he downed the last drop of the magic brew, he felt decidedly better and actually admitted that Kirby had a point. He *had* asked for her help. But not because he needed it, for heaven's sake. Another motive altogether had prompted his request.

And rigid schedules such as the one she'd made were for people with productivity problems, people who didn't know how to manage their time. He'd juggled two careers for years. He had no such worries.

So why doesn't Jason have his book? Matt's conscience immediately demanded.

He gulped and glanced toward the living room again. From all appearances, Kirby Lee Gibson knew her stuff. In fact, she'd had a lot of good—if somewhat impractical—ideas the night before. What harm could there possibly be in humoring her this week?

Besides, even spending time with a Fury beat the heck out of spending time alone—especially when the Fury was as sexy as this one was.

Maybe if he begged, she would have a little pity and let him stay.

Begged? "Macho" Matt Foxx?

Matt groaned his disgust at his weakness where Kirby was concerned. Why he found a woman who was so opposite so darned irresistible, he really couldn't imagine. Was it his nonexistent social life, the solitude of the cabin, the talk with his grandmother?

Or was it destiny?

"Destiny, hell," he muttered with an incredulous laugh, setting his coffee mug on the counter and heading to the living room.

Kirby never even looked up when Matt joined her in the middle of the room where she knelt, neatly folding the contents of his suitcase so she could close it.

"Uh, Kirby?"

"Umm?"

"I-I'm sorry I was such a jerk a while ago. I really do appreciate your efforts to civilize me."

"Hmph!"

"No, really," Matt declared, dropping to one knee beside her. He gave her his most earnest smile. "And though I said I didn't want your help, I really didn't mean it."

That got her attention. Sitting back on her heels, Kirby met his gaze square on. "Are you saying you want to stay and try the schedule?"

Matt nodded eagerly. "Exactly."

Kirby hesitated, as though trying to weigh his sincerity, then shook her head and went back to work. "Forget it. We'll never be on the same wavelength."

"Sure, we will. Just look at the progress you've made with me so far."

"Progress?" she echoed in obvious disbelief, meeting his gaze again. "What progress?"

"I ate breakfast, didn't I?"

"I hardly think a bit of toast and a spoonful of oatmeal qualifies as breakfast." Kirby began to fold his clothes again.

Matt caught her face in his hands, forcing her to stop and look at him. "It's a start. Pl-e-a-s-e?"

"No!" she exclaimed, tugging his hands away.

"Aw, come on," he urged. "Where's your patience? I admit I've been a horse's rear this morning, but only because I hadn't had my second cup of coffee. Surely you've had resistant clients before."

"Tons of them," Kirby agreed. "And I usually handle them well. Frankly, Matt, something about you irritates the holy heck out of me."

"Ditto," he murmured. "But I still don't want to leave. Why do you suppose that is?"

"I really don't know," Kirby replied, suddenly getting to her feet. She walked over to the fire and tossed on another log. "I do know that all this bickering is getting me down. ''Tis the season to be jolly,' Matt."

"So 'tis." Matt got to his feet and walked over to the window. Pulling back the curtain, he looked out on a winter wonderland.

Beautiful, he thought, at once filled with the peace he usually found when close to nature—peace that had eluded him for eight weeks. Why now? he wondered in amazement. Why *now* such peace and such a consuming sense of rightness?

Did it have something to do with Kirby's arrival? he wondered with a thoughtful glance in her direction. He realized she was looking at him and turned toward the window again, his head spinning with dozens of questions but only one clear answer: destiny.

Destiny. That word again. Matt frowned and reluctantly gave it some serious consideration.

He'd always believed that some things happened because they were meant to—his writing, for example. Could it be that this cabin mix-up was actually one of those predestined occurrences? That Kirby really had been sent to the cabin, not by the Fates, Muses or Venus, but for a reason, all the same?

Was she—he gulped back rising panic—was she the woman of his most secret dreams, the woman who would desire him not for his money and life-style, but in spite of it?

"What do you see out there?" Kirby's question barely penetrated his frantic speculation.

"Oh, um, I see snow...ice...." He noted a sudden splash of color marring the white landscape. "Freddie Fox."

"Excuse me?"

Abruptly Matt realized he'd uttered aloud the name he'd impulsively given the red fox who visited the cabin almost every day—a name he'd stolen from his own Skeeter Skunk novels. He winced. "I said 'a friendly fox.'"

"No, you didn't." Kirby joined him at the window, but instead of looking outside, stepped right in front, forcing him to look at her. "You said Freddie Fox." Her eyes sparkled with mirth. "Does that mean you're a Skeeter Skunk fan, too?"

His jaw dropped. "Too? *You* read them?"

She nodded. "Aloud. On Saturdays. To kids at the library." She cocked her head to one side. "What's your excuse?"

How Matt would've loved to blurt, "I write them." But he couldn't—not to the sister-in-law of the publisher who'd worked so hard to create and maintain the playboy image of Matt Foxx.

"I read them to my nieces and nephews." That *was* true.

"Oh."

She turned then and put her nose to the frosty windowpane. "Where is ol' Freddie?"

Matt stepped closer and peered out over her head. "Don't see him now, but he'll be back. I've been leaving meat scraps on the porch for him."

Laughing, Kirby turned—and found her nose touching Matt's chest...that oh-so-touchable chest. She tipped her head back and exchanged a heart-stopping glance with him, then slipped past...or tried to. Since Matt suddenly placed his hands on the window frame on either side of her, she didn't get far.

"What say we call a truce?" he asked, his voice husky soft, his eyes pleading.

Kirby abruptly ceased her efforts to escape. Her heart kick-started again—double time. "Think we can? We're opposites, you know."

"I know, but I honestly believe we have enough in common to share a roof for a few days and live to tell about it."

"Name one thing we have in common," she challenged.

"We both like Skeeter Skunk books," Matt said, hastily adding, "You *do* like them, don't you?"

"I love them."

He heaved a sigh of relief. "And so do I. See? I told you we had something in common."

"If that's the only thing, we're in big trouble," Kirby told him. "Somehow I think a mature relationship should be based on more than mutual respect for Skeeter Skunk."

"Did you say 'relationship'?"

Kirby's heart stopped again. "If I did, I didn't mean to."

"What did you mean to say?" he asked, his question fanning the wisp of bangs feathered over her forehead.

Kirby pressed her back to the window. "*Friendship.* I think friends should have more than one little thing in common."

"There are other things."

"Like what?"

"We both like jeans." He leaned back slightly and dropped his gaze to hers, smiling appreciatively.

Kirby squirmed. "Name something else."

"Red." He shifted his gaze to her sweater, where it lingered, as intimate as a caress.

Kirby shivered.

"Are you cold?"

"Well, my backside *is* as good as stuck out the window."

"Come over by the fire," he said. "I'll warm you up."

Since that's just what Kirby was afraid of, she shook her head a little too vigorously from side to side. "Not until you tell me something else we have in common instead."

"If I do, will you agree to that truce and never, ever mention sending me packing again?"

"Yes."

"Okay, then." To Kirby's relief, Matt stepped back and stuffed his fingers in his pockets. He began to pace the room, frowning, obviously deep in thought. Kirby actually began to wonder if he were going to be able to come up with anything.

She realized with a start that she hoped so—she sincerely hoped so.

What is wrong with me? Kirby asked herself. Where was her sensible head? Her sensible heart? Why was she suddenly questioning years of common sense and moral living and actually wondering if her mother's philosophy was the right one after all: If he makes you feel good, then keep him . . . whether or not you agree with his life-style, political affiliation or, in this case, main character?

Suddenly Matt halted his march. He turned to her, clearly baffled. "I'm afraid I'm stumped."

"What about the orange juice?" Kirby heard herself blurt. "We both like that."

Matt's face lit up. "Yeah, we do, don't we?"

"And grandmothers. We're partial to those."

"Uh-huh, and sisters."

Kirby wrinkled her nose. "Sometimes."

Matt laughed, and to her surprise, closed the distance between them to engulf her in his arms. "I think I like you, Kirby Lee Gibson—opposite or no. Do you like me?"

Warmed by his declaration and the innocent embrace, Kirby found herself hugging him back.

"You know . . . I believe I do," she confessed. "I believe I do . . . God forbid."

Chapter Four

Matt grinned and set her free by lowering his arms. "And there we have it, folks," he announced with a grin. "The 'Miracle on Gibson Ridge,' which surely rivals the one on Thirty-fourth Street, I might add."

Kirby put precious inches between them. "Don't tell me the author of *Freedom Four*, *Murder in Madrid*, and *The Scapegoat* likes that sentimental old movie?"

"But of course he does. What about the woman who believes too much television is bad for her eyes?"

"Of course she does," Kirby replied.

"Something else we have in common!" he exclaimed. "This is absolutely amazing and solid proof that we're going to have smooth sailing from now on." He walked over to plop down on the couch.

Why don't I believe you? Somewhat more slowly, Kirby joined him, her thoughts on her mother for the second time that morning. Kirby well remembered the pain that had resulted when that parent repeatedly followed her heart instead of her head. Was her oldest daughter now following in those footsteps? Did heartache lurk ahead?

Lost in sudden gloom at the mere idea, Kirby silently sank into the chair.

"What's wrong?" Matt asked, obviously picking up on her mood. "Second thoughts already?"

"No," Kirby lied. "I'm just wondering what we're going to do now."

"Whatever's on that schedule of yours," he replied, leaning back, crossing his arms over his ample chest, seemingly prepared for whatever she might dish out to him.

"First on the agenda is finding a shirt for you," Kirby said, determined not to be distracted by that— or any other—part of his anatomy again. "Are they all dirty or something?"

"No. I just felt like going without." He glanced down at his upper torso. "And still do...unless you have an objection."

"Not really," Kirby lied. "I just can't help thinking you must be cold...."

"Naw."

Well, darn.

"So now that we've settled that, what *is* next?"

"Work. How many chapters do you have to write before you mail this book of yours to Jason?"

"Ten and a half."

"And they're due on his desk when?"

"Christmas."

She whistled softly. "Thank goodness I showed up when I did. Someone certainly needs to teach you how to condition your creativity to come when called. Follow me."

With determined steps, Kirby led the way to the kitchen. Matt rose with reluctance and dragged his feet all the way.

"Okay, now sit," Kirby instructed when he joined her at the word processor.

Matt did as requested, settling himself into the chair. He stared at the screen, hoping it wouldn't look this blank when he finished for the day.

"Now, I don't want you to get up from there until you've produced five pages. You can take a short break then."

Five pages? From a has-been? Matt wanted to laugh…or was it cry? "First I've got to turn this thing on." He flipped a switch on the back of his computer and listened to the familiar whir, remembering a time when he'd loved that sound, a time when his fingers itched to put words to screen. Now he actually dreaded it.

"All set," he reported to Kirby seconds later when he called up the page he'd worked on last.

"What's that jerk, Ross Elliot, up to now?" she asked, peering over his shoulder at the monitor.

"Nothing," he grumbled, every bit as irritated by her question as his expected lack of inspiration. "That's why I'm here."

"May I ask you a personal question?"

Anything to keep from writing. "I may not answer it."

"Fair enough." She thought for a moment, then cleared her throat. "Would you say you were exactly like your main character, similar to your main character, or opposite to your main character?"

"In other words, are all the tabloids right about me?"

"I suppose you could put it that way."

"You *know* I could put it that way," he snapped in annoyance. Couldn't she *tell* what kind of man he was, dammit? Did he dare risk all by spelling it out to her?

"So what's your answer?"

"I'm pleading the fifth," Matt said, deciding it would be best not to tell her the truth until he knew exactly how close she was to her brother-in-law. All he needed was for Jason to hear that the creator of world-famous Ross Elliot had also created Skeeter Skunk, Freddie Fox and Rosalie Rabbit. Matt ducked his shoulder from under her chin and swiveled in the chair so that he faced her. "You don't really expect me to write with you standing there, do you?"

Kirby winced, then gave him a sheepish smile. "Sorry. Why don't I just make myself scarce?"

"Why don't you?"

Humming "We Wish You a Merry Christmas," she left Matt to his current project, a political suspense novel entitled *The Cairo Connection*. As with every other time he'd sat at this table the past eight weeks, Matt's inspiration immediately vanished to parts unknown.

He stared at the words on the screen, most of which he'd written back in Seattle before Jason sentenced him to the solitude of this mountain hideaway. It was almost as though someone besides Matt had created the premise and completed the first fourteen chapters of this novel. He didn't know his plot or his characters anymore. Worse than that, he didn't even know how the darned thing was supposed to end.

"Hell," Matt muttered in utter disgust, shaking his head. At that moment he heard what sounded like Kirby scooting furniture in the next room. Already bored with the assignment she'd given him, he tipped his chair back on two legs so he could peer through the door into the living room to see what she was up to.

He could see nothing from where he sat and, reluctant to get up without typing anything, Matt turned his attention back to his would-be bestseller.

Matt reread what he'd written of the chapter so far, changing a word here and there. He decided it wasn't half as bad as he'd thought and actually felt faint stirrings of what might be inspiration.

Maybe she's done it, he thought, at once greatly encouraged. *Maybe this lamebrained schedule of hers is actually going to work.* Matt put his fingers to the keyboard and...froze, his mind once again a vacuum.

Next door Kirby sang "O' Christmas Tree" to the accompaniment of bumps and thuds that told Matt she was still at work. Doing what, he couldn't imagine, and since *that* intrigued him more than *this,* he got to his feet and walked to the door to look into the living room.

All he saw was Kirby's temptingly rounded backside and shapely legs, since she now stood on a step stool and everything above the waist was out of sight in the closet. Matt relished the view—he'd become a connoisseur of late—and wondered what color panties she wore this day.

The fact that Kirby's lingerie intrigued him more than his unfinished novel astounded Matt. His writing had been his driving force for years. Why, just yesterday his iffy future as an author had consumed his thoughts. Today he couldn't seem to care whether or not he ever wrote again.

Instead, he wanted nothing more than to research the color of Kirby's undies.

Did that mean there was actually merit to his earlier conjectures? Was she indeed the woman of his dreams? It sure looked that way. Why else would he be so enchanted by her? But until he knew for sure, he would have to keep his mind off Kirby's underwear so he could keep his hands to himself. He didn't want to frighten her off . . . just in case.

Matt chuckled softly, acknowledging that keeping his hands to himself should be easy enough. Ms. Sensible would never do anything so spontaneous as to fool around with the likes of him. He guessed that when she gave herself, it would be for keeps and only because she believed she'd found *her* destiny.

And that was his answer, of course.

If he pursued her and got nowhere, he would know she was not *the one*. If he pursued and won her, especially in light of the "bad" reputation she'd quizzed him about . . .

At once Matt's stomach did a back-flip that told him he might not be quite ready to win her. True, he'd always intended to settle down just as his beloved nana had suggested, but he hadn't planned on its being quite so soon or with such an opposite.

He wasn't at all sure he was ready for that kind of challenge—destiny or no.

Just then Kirby stepped off her stool and staggered under her load, a long pasteboard box. Resisting the urge to come to her aid, Matt watched her lug the box to a spot she'd cleared near the window. She placed it beside another box, this one smaller, then extracted the green plastic branches of an artificial Christmas tree.

Horrified, Matt abruptly abandoned all conjectures of forever after and pursuit, not to mention his book.

"What do you think you're doing?" he demanded, storming into the room.

Kirby started violently and dropped the branch she was inserting into the "trunk" of the tree. Glaring at Matt, she promptly scooped it up again. "To your left sits a chest full of ornaments and to your right, what will soon be a pine tree. What do *you* think I'm doing?"

"Not in *my* cabin, you don't."

Kirby's eyes rounded. "You don't put up a Christmas tree?"

"Not a plastic one. They're un-American."

"No, they're not," Kirby retorted. "They're practical. Artificial trees are perfectly shaped, are always green and are not a fire hazard." She sounded as though she recited a hard-learned lesson.

Matt snorted his disagreement. "They're un-American," he repeated. "Especially when you're surrounded by acres of forest. I've never had a fake tree. I don't intend to start now." With that, he snatched the branches she held, crammed them back into the box along with the pole that served as tree trunk and shut the flaps.

"Matt!"

Ignoring Kirby's protest, Matt yanked coats, a hat and gloves from the hall tree. He tossed hers over with a brisk "Put them on," then headed to his suitcase for a flannel shirt. After donning it, he pulled on his boots, his leather gloves and then his jacket.

When he finished, he turned to find that Kirby still sat among her boxes, watching him in astonishment. Snorting his impatience, Matt crossed over and pulled her to her feet. While she sputtered her objections, he dressed her in her furry jacket, her brown wool gloves and the matching stocking cap, which he playfully pulled down over her eyes.

Kirby screeched her outrage and swung her gloved fist at him, a punch easily dodged by a laughing Matt. He herded her toward the door, only to halt when he realized she stood in her socks.

"Don't move," he ordered as he headed to the bedroom for the leather boots that had almost been his demise the day before. When he returned to the living room seconds later, he found that Kirby had yanked off the cap and one of the gloves.

Matt lunged. Kirby squealed and tried to run, but managed only one step before Matt ducked his shoulder into her midsection and lifted her right off her feet. With difficulty—one hand still held the boots, and the other was draped over the flailing legs of his irate hostess—Matt opened the front door and stepped out onto the porch.

He breathed deeply of the invigorating mountain air and smiled his appreciation of God's glorious handiwork. "Gorgeous, isn't it?"

"How would I know?" Kirby snapped. From her upside-down vantage point, all she could see was her hair, which hung like a veil around her face, and Matt's butt, which she would definitely kick first chance she got.

"If I put you down, will you behave?" he asked.

"Yes," she lied, fully intending to dash back inside and lock the door. Only after he begged for mercy would she let him in, and maybe not even then.

"Okay," he said, but to her astonishment he did not set her on her feet. Instead, he stepped off the porch and dumped her there in the clearing next to her car, flat on her back in the snow. Next, he dropped her boots beside her and picked up an ax from where it lay next to the wood piled on the porch. "Hurry up," he ordered as he stomped over to examine a small pine tree. "Looks like it's going to snow again."

Plotting revenge for her humiliation, Kirby quickly pulled on her boots, then the glove and hat she'd somehow managed to hang on to. She toyed with the idea of making a run for the cabin and locking Matt outside as originally planned, but decided against it. He would most likely tear the place down trying to get back in.

Obviously she was going to have to go with him to get his stupid old tree, something she could definitely, but definitely, live without...and no wonder. The one

other time she'd celebrated Christmas with a real tree
had been a total disaster, and she didn't want to be reminded of it now.

Kirby got slowly to her feet and brushed the snow
off her jeans and jacket. She noted that Matt, criti-
cally eyeing tree after tree, still had his back to her and
mischievously scooped up a huge handful of the pow-
dery snow. After forming it into a massive ball as best
she could, she edged her way over to where her unsuspecting housemate stood.

"Matt?"

The moment he spun round, Kirby threw the snowball, which splattered all over his face. He roared his
surprise and indignation. Kirby howled her glee...
until she realized he intended to reciprocate.

With a gasp, she began to run, not easy in knee-deep
snow. Matt, with his longer legs, caught up seconds
later and washed her face thoroughly in the frosty
fluff.

Laughing, she slapped him away and scrambled to
gather up enough snow to fight back. Before she could
attempt to pat it into a ball, however, Matt tackled her
and they fell to the snow-cushioned ground together.

Laughing like crazy, they tussled in the snow. They
could have been children—best friends without a care
in the world—or even lovers—two people who would
soon run inside to the warmth of the fire and each
other.

How tempting that scenario, Kirby thought even as
Matt pushed her over on her back and then immobi-
lized her with the entire length of his massive body.

Kirby's hormones simmered in response, and she fully expected the snow to melt and then boil beneath her.

"Let me up," she gasped, trying to push him off.

"First you have to say 'uncle,'" Matt responded, brushing his fingers over her breasts in his attempt to capture her hands. An accident? she wondered, suddenly so distracted that he actually succeeded and pinned her wrists to his racing heart.

"And if I refuse?"

"I'll be forced to hold you here forever."

"Sweet temptation."

Only when Matt tensed did Kirby realize she'd uttered her crazy thought aloud. How scandalous. How wanton. *How embarrassing*. Face flaming, Kirby closed her eyes to block out his piercing blue gaze. She wished with all her heart she could just crawl under this blanket of snow and never, ever come out again.

"Kirby?"

"What?"

"Look at me."

She did, oh-so-reluctantly.

"It's snowing."

Surprised by the unexpected comment, Kirby peeked over his shoulder. "Yes."

"As I see it, we have two options. We can either carry this conversation inside now and finish it stretched out in front of the fireplace, or we can go on and get our Christmas tree and *then* stretch out."

He called those options? If *that* wasn't a Ross Elliot attitude, she'd eat her fuzzy wool cap!

"As much as I want to stretch out with you—and, honey, I'm wanting—" he smoothly continued, "I'm thinking we'd better go get that tree first. If the weathermen are right, this may be our last chance for a safe trek in the woods."

"I have a better idea," Kirby said, suddenly as sobered by the reality of the threatening bad weather as the idea of "stretching out" with Matt Foxx. "Let's end this conversation right here and now, go inside and put up the artificial tree."

"No way," Matt exclaimed, levering himself up and reaching out to tug her to her feet. He quickly brushed his body free of its dusting of snow, then helped Kirby. His hands again lingering where they shouldn't, seemed to confirm Kirby's earlier suspicions. Thoroughly exasperated, she pushed him away.

Any man would do what any woman would let him ... whether he really liked her or not. That was a rule every mother—or in this case, grandmother—drilled into the brains of their teenaged daughters.

Matt Foxx was no exception. In fact, he was probably the reason for the damned rule. And if he'd taken liberties today, it was only to see how far she would let him go and not because he really wanted her.

It was high time to regain control of this situation, Kirby realized, glaring at her companion. In fact, it was *past* time.

Seemingly oblivious to her quandary, Matt retrieved the ax he'd tossed aside when they began their foolishness moments ago. He tucked the handle of it into the tooled leather belt he wore. "Ready?"

Before Kirby could respond, Matt grabbed her gloved hand in his and practically dragged her into the woods surrounding the cabin.

"This looks like a good one," he commented several yards later, halting in front of what had to be the scraggliest tree on the mountain.

Kirby immediately nixed his selection. "You've got to be kidding."

Matt arched an eyebrow in what Kirby suspected might be feigned surprise. "What's wrong with it?"

"It's way too short. And look...it's one-sided." She flicked a glance his way and shrugged. "Not that I really care, you understand. But if you have to do this, at least do it right."

"Whatever you say." Matt glanced around and then walked over to a tree equally unsuitable. "How about this one?"

"For crying out loud," Kirby groaned. "That one's worse than the other one. Come on. I'll find one that'll look right in the living room."

With a decidedly smug smile, Matt stepped back to give her the lead. With difficulty, she forged a path through the icy brambles, vines and underbrush, and just missed stepping on a snow-covered something she could not at first identify. Then she cried out her alarm. Matt caught up with her in two long strides.

"Look," she exclaimed, clutching his arm with one hand, pointing with the other. Matt registered her distress, then shifted his gaze to the source of it—a trap, placed there in the snow to capture some poor, unsuspecting creature. Clearly as furious as Kirby, he tore a limb from a fallen log and rammed it into the trap, which snapped shut with a vengeance. Kirby flinched at the wicked sound.

Matt pulled the trap up from the frozen ground and stashed it far inside the hollow log, out of harm's way.

"Do you think there are more?" Kirby asked, looking at the ground all around. Tears of anger blinded her, one of which snaked its way down her burning cheek.

To Kirby's surprise, Matt captured her chin in his fingers and then leaned forward to catch that salty drop with his lips. A heartbeat later those lips covered hers, and all thoughts of Freddie Fox, the trap and even her irresponsible mother vanished in the thin mountain air.

Matt tugged her closer, his hands cupping her bottom to hold her tightly to him. The warmth of him quickly permeated her body, heating her simmering hormones way past boiling right on up to danger point. Kirby—cold-natured Kirby—actually felt sweat trickle down the valley between her breasts.

When Matt slipped his hand under her jacket and palmed one of those tingling breasts through her sweater, she knew for certain he knew exactly what he was doing. No accident, this.

Kirby also knew she should protest, and she actually tried to. But Matt's kiss stole the words, and his magic hands her will to utter them.

Am I my mother's daughter, after all? she agonized, almost losing that thought as she melted into his touch. Could any man set me on fire this way? Or just this one? Is Matt Foxx my...

...*destiny?* The word exploded in Matt's head yet again, and its reappearance shocked him right to the heated core. Was he going, going, gone... already? And without so much as a protest? At once as shaken by his thoughts as by the potency of the unexpected kiss, Matt abruptly released Kirby.

Warily they exchanged a soul-searching look. Matt could see her bewilderment and guessed she took new measure of him, just as he took new measure of her.

"Thanks for saving Freddie Fox," Kirby said, her voice a mere whisper in the crisp winter wind.

"Saving...? Oh, the trap." So she thought he'd done it for the fox. Well, he would have, if it had crossed his mind. As it was, her own near miss had enraged him to action, and even now he shuddered at the thought of what could have happened had she stepped in the trap herself. "I don't believe in killing for any reason other than to put food on the table."

"Maybe you aren't as much like Ross Elliot as I thought," she commented. "Maybe you *are* a nice man."

"Didn't I tell you so?" he retorted, adding, "And just for the record, you're pretty doggone nice yourself."

Kirby sighed lustily. "I suppose that's better than compulsive."

"I did call you that, didn't I?"

"Yes." Her eyes suddenly lit up. "You wouldn't call me that now?"

"I probably would," he said with a grin. "But I will take back what I said about your body."

"Excuse me?"

"You do have a spontaneous bone—maybe even two."

"So *that's* what you were groping around for a minute ago!" she exclaimed. "A spontaneous bone."

Matt winced. So she'd noticed the way his hands seemed to have a mind of their own, or, now that he thought of it, a hot line to his innermost desires. "Uh-huh."

"Well, you won't find one *there*."

"Oh." He faked a pout, then pretended to be inspired by a new plan. "May I try somewhere else, then? There's a lot more of you I'd love to explore."

She gasped, truly shocked, which delighted him. "You certainly may not. If you search for anything, it's going to be a Christmas tree. That *is* what we came out here for."

"Oh, yeah." Matt tore his gaze from the blushing woman before him and glanced around. Snow now fell in earnest and showed no signs of letting up. Matt noted that their tracks were already covered. "We'd better hurry," he said, at once all business. "Keep the cabin in sight at all times."

Kirby nodded, instantly as serious as he. Together they began anew their search, and since their minds were on their quest this time, they found the perfect tree shortly after.

At least ten feet tall and beautifully formed, the Douglas fir they selected soon toppled to the ground at their feet. Together they carried it back to the cabin porch, where they shook it free of snow and ice.

Getting it into the cabin took some maneuvering, and getting it upright proved as big a challenge. Matt did most of the work—supervised by Kirby, of course. And an hour slipped by before they found their tree and finally stood back to admire its fragrant, blue-green beauty.

Matt grinned his satisfaction with a job well done. He loved everything about Christmas from the candy canes to the carols—always had. And special memories now warmed him.

He glanced at Kirby, trying to decipher her expression. Did fond thoughts of long ago fill her head, too? he wondered. As though she could feel his gaze on her, Kirby turned. She gave him a sweet smile he felt to the marrow.

Relishing the fragile peace, Matt closed the distance between them and draped an arm across her shoulders. He gave her a little hug. "Now aren't you glad I talked you out of that plastic excuse for a tree?"

Kirby elbowed his ribs. "I'll have you know that 'plastic excuse for a tree' served my grandmother well for years."

Matt shook his head. "I can't believe that the owner of all these acres of woods would actually put up an artificial tree."

"My grandmother was so environmentally conscious that she wouldn't have burned trees for heat if we could have afforded to do it another way. She'd never have killed a tree just so we could hang ornaments on it." Kirby looked heavenward, murmuring, "Sorry, Nana. I promise to plant another."

"And I'll help her," Matt solemnly interjected, never doubting for a moment that Kirby's nana could hear them.

Obviously bemused that Matt would join in a conversation with her deceased grandmother, Kirby reached out to touch a branch of the fir. "It really is quite lovely, isn't it?"

"Just wait until we get the decorations on it," Matt told her.

"What do you mean 'we'? Don't you have a book to write?"

"That can wait until this afternoon. Right now I'm going to help you decorate the tree."

Though Matt half expected Kirby to argue, she said nothing. Dropping to her knees beside the smaller of the two boxes she'd taken from the closet, she began dragging out all shapes and sizes of decorations, most of them the glittery plastic variety.

Matt winced at the sight. "What are you going to do with that stuff?"

Kirby sat back and sent him a pitying look. "Hang them on the branches, of course."

"Oh, no, you don't. Nothing but homemade decorations are going to be hung on this baby."

Kirby sucked in a hissing breath, then got slowly to her feet. "There is no reason for either of us to waste time making decorations when these will do just fine."

"But that's the fun part—"

"You're here to write a book, not have fun."

Matt glared at her but said nothing. Turning on his heel, he stomped to the kitchen.

Inordinately pleased at how skillfully she'd maneuvered him to get back to business, Kirby knelt in front of the box again. *It's all a matter of assertiveness,* she told herself as she reached for a red plastic ornament. Suddenly the sounds of a clash and a clang emanated from the kitchen.

Baffled—she'd never heard a computer make a noise like that—Kirby leapt up and made tracks in that direction. She peeked through the door, immediately spotting Matt, who stood at the stove, his hand on the handle of a huge cooking pot.

"What are you doing?" Kirby demanded.

"Popping corn to string for the tree," he replied without batting an eye. "Do you think three bowls will be enough?"

Chapter Five

"Do I think...? Oh, Matt!" Kirby barely resisted her impulse to strangle him. "You're unbelievable, you know that?"

Matt said nothing—just kept his eyes on the covered pan, the handle of which he clutched in a white-knuckled grip.

"Don't you even want to finish your book?" Kirby demanded.

"You know I do."

"Then why on earth don't you sit down and get on with it?"

"*Because I can't!*" Matt yelled. He sucked in a deep breath and then slowly exhaled it, visibly struggling for composure. "I can't. I've lost it, Kirby...lost it."

Startled by his emotional outburst, Kirby had no reply. She noted Matt's flushed cheeks, the anguished glint in his blue eyes, which would not meet hers.

Suddenly she saw more than a fun-loving playboy who wrote novels on the side. She saw a serious professional with several bestsellers to his credit, who, for some unknown reason, couldn't finish his current project.

Her tender heart went out to him.

"Why don't you pop four bowls of corn?" she said. "We'll have the extra for lunch. It's a good source of fiber." With that, Kirby spun on her heel and walked back toward the living room, pausing just before she stepped through the door. She turned slightly, and upon finding Matt watching her exit in obvious astonishment, mustered a reassuring smile. "Maybe you're trying too hard. Maybe if you just relax, the words will come."

A second later, alone in the living room, Kirby tried to lift her own suddenly drooping spirits by humming "Santa Claus Is Coming to Town" and delving into her box of decorations, some of which she knew were handmade and would therefore meet Matt's standards.

She found dozens of snowflakes, five candy canes, six snowmen and two miniature stockings, all of which her nana had crocheted from colorful yarn. She also found a cornshuck angel they'd bought at a craft fair years ago.

With only half a mind, Kirby lovingly examined each ornament. With the other half, she worried about the man in the kitchen. What could have happened to bring so talented a writer to this sad state of affairs? And why this unexpected, unwanted sympathy for him?

Was it because they really were the "friends" they claimed to be? Or did more than friendly feelings produce this ache, this anxiety for him?

Several minutes and no brilliant insights later, Kirby gave up trying to decipher her motives and followed her nose back to the stove, from whence a mouth-watering aroma now emanated.

Just as she entered the kitchen, Matt dumped a steaming panful of the fluffy white kernels into a brown paper sack, the sides of which he had rolled down a couple of times, probably to keep it open.

He reached for the salt shaker, a move that must have put Kirby in his line of vision, for he halted before salting and arched an eyebrow in a silent quest for permission.

"Lightly," she said, adding, "Please."

Matt rolled his eyes as though exasperated, but the twinkle in them told her he didn't really mind cooperating. After salting, he got back to business. Kirby watched him work and relished the presence of the easy smile that had replaced his frown.

Impulsively she slipped behind him, locked her arms around his waist and pressed her cheek to his back, just about heart high. Before he could react to her hug of sympathy and understanding, Kirby stepped away and scooped up a handful of popped corn, which she munched as though nothing had just transpired between them.

Matt eyed her warily for a long moment, but made no comment. Instead, he turned his attention back to popping three more pans full, and he filled the sack to overflowing before he stopped.

They then carried the corn to the living room and set it on the rug in front of the fireplace. While Kirby hunted up thread and needles, Matt added a log to the blaze.

"How come your grandmother never put central heating in this old cabin?" he asked when he finished and settled himself on the rug, his long legs stretched out in front of him, his back propped against the couch.

"She claimed it would cost too much," Kirby replied. Sewing basket in hand, she sat on the rug near his feet, her back to the chair. "But I've always thought she was just too sentimental to modernize the place any more than she had to. My great-great-grandpa built it over a hundred years ago for him and his new bride."

"No kidding?"

"No kidding. He later gave it to my great-grandpa on *his* wedding day and so on down the line. This roof has sheltered five generations of Gibsons."

"I knew there was something special about this place the minute I set foot in it," Matt murmured, reaching for the needle and thread Kirby handed to him. He glanced around the room, his thoughtful gaze lingering here and then there. "Just think of the dreams that have come true within these walls." He focused his attention on Kirby. "Your nana was your mother's mother, right?"

PLAY THE
LUCKY
CARNIVAL WHEEL
scratch-off game
and get as many as
SIX FREE GIFTS . . .

HOW TO PLAY:

1. With a coin, carefully scratch off the silver area at right. Then check your number against the chart below it to find out which gifts you're eligible to receive.

2. You'll receive brand-new Silhouette Romance™ novels and possibly other gifts—ABSOLUTELY FREE! Send back this card and we'll promptly send you the free books and gifts you qualify for!

3. We're betting you'll want more of these heart-warming romances, so unless you tell us otherwise, every month we'll send you 6 more wonderful novels to read and enjoy. Always delivered right to your home. And always at a discount off the cover price!

4. Your satisfaction is guaranteed! You may return any shipment of books and cancel at any time. The Free Books and Gifts remain yours to keep!

NO COST! NO RISK!
NO OBLIGATION TO BUY!

You'll look like a million dollars when you wear this elegant necklace! It's a generous 20 inches long and each link is double-soldered for strength and durability.

More Good News For Subscribers-Only!

When you join the Silhouette Reader Service™, you'll receive 6 heart-warming romance novels each month delivered to your home. You'll also get additional free gifts from time to time as well as our subscribers-only newsletter. It's your privileged look at upcoming books and profiles of our most popular authors!

If offer card is missing, write to:
Silhouette Reader Service, 3010 Walden Avenue, P.O. Box 1867, Buffalo, NY 14269-1867

"That's right." Sensing he was about to ask questions she might not want to answer, Kirby stuck her freshly threaded needle through a piece of the popped corn and motioned for Matt to get busy, too.

"Was your mother an only child?" he asked, obediently setting to work handily stringing one fluffy kernel after another.

"Yes," Kirby replied.

"So the Gibson name dies with this generation."

"I'm still a Gibson."

"Surely it's only a matter of time until you find the right man and change your name," Matt said. "Just like your sister did."

"Unfortunately my sister did not find the right man. She married for love. I intend to marry sensibly."

You would, Matt thought, though he said nothing aloud. Instead, he picked up a piece of popcorn, which he tossed into the air and caught in his mouth. He grinned when he saw that Kirby was properly impressed, and decided to make the most of this wonderful opportunity to examine her relationship to the man Madison married for love—a man who just happened to be his publisher.

"Jason Lawrence is a well-respected, successful, *rich* man. I should think any mama would be proud to have him for a son-in-law and any sister for a brother-in-law. Why don't you like him?"

"It's not that I don't like him," Kirby said, a reply that told Matt he'd best forget once and for all this persistent impulse to come clean with her. "I do...well enough to tolerate him, at least. He's just so darned arrogant and so into *things*... clothes, his sports car, their new house. And he's always trying to fix me up with this or that someone just like him.'' She shuddered as though she found the idea repulsive.

That pleased Matt, who didn't like his sudden vision of Kirby surrounded by a bunch of adoring yuppies. ''I admit Jason does have an oversized ego. But he really isn't so bad once you get used to him.''

''Of course *you'd* think that. You're probably just as bad as he is.''

Matt nearly choked. Biting back the confession that still threatened to tumble off his tongue, he managed a casual shrug designed to give away nothing. He clasped both ends of his popcorn string and stretched it out. ''How long should this thing be?''

''A lot longer than that,'' Kirby replied. She looked a little peeved, whether because Matt hadn't denied her comparison or because she guessed he was already bored with his current task, she couldn't be sure. ''Stringing popcorn *was* your idea.''

''And a marvelous one, I might add.'' He glanced at the tree, trying to picture it adorned with popcorn strands and... Matt frowned. What else? he suddenly wondered. ''I don't suppose you brought any cranberries with you...?''

''Not the kind you hang on trees, if that's what you're asking.''

''That's what I'm asking,'' he replied, disappointed. ''We need some color on those branches. Got any of those little bitty lights—the kind that blink on and off?''

''Lights? On *this* tree? Isn't that sacrilege?''

"Lights are a must on any tree," Matt assured her. At that, he got to his feet and walked over to Kirby's box of decorations. Beside it, he spotted a neat stack of crocheted ornaments. Momentarily distracted from his mission, Matt knelt and examined each. "These are really nice," he commented, holding up a snow-flake crocheted from white yarn through which a slender gold thread had been woven. "Who made them?"

"Nana," Kirby said, walking over to join him. "She was very clever." She dropped to one knee beside him and dug into the decoration box. She located the re-quested string of lights and handed it to Matt.

He took the lights without complaint, making short work of looping them around the tree, top to bottom. When he stepped back to survey his handiwork, Kirby tied a snowflake on a branch. Then she added an-other. Matt quickly followed suit, carefully position-ing his share of the ornaments so that they were evenly distributed all over the tree.

As soon as they finished, Kirby herded Matt back to the popcorn. They sat in front of the fireplace for over an hour afterward, alternately eating and string-ing the popcorn while they talked about whatever en-tered their heads.

The clock said twelve-thirty when they finally draped the yards-long string around the tree and placed the angel on top. Matt plugged in the lights and again stepped back to get the full effect.

"Still needs color," he murmured. "Got any red balls in that box?"

"Yes," she said, with a teasing smile adding, "But they're not homemade."

"Just so they're real glass," he retorted, retrieving three crimson-colored balls from the box. "I hate those plastic ones."

Kirby smiled in response and added two blue balls and a silver one of her own. This time they both stepped away for a better perspective of their tree, which positively glowed in the dim interior of the cabin.

"Perfect," Matt said.

"It is pretty, isn't it?" Kirby let Matt lead her to the couch, where they sat on opposite ends, their gazes still on the tree. Silence reigned for several minutes before Matt looked her way. To his astonishment, he saw her brush away a tear.

At once concerned that he'd somehow hurt Kirby by insisting on a real tree, Matt scooted over, closing the distance between them.

"What's wrong?" he asked, draping his arm across the back of the couch. To his surprise, she snuggled against him, one arm draped across his chest. Absently he fingered a strand of her hair, shimmering like spun gold in the flickering firelight.

Kirby laughed softly, a self-conscious sound to his ears. "Sorry, I was just remembering the last time I had a real tree at Christmas. I was probably twelve... or maybe thirteen." She said nothing for a moment, clearly lost in her memories, then murmured, "Yeah, thirteen."

"I'd like to hear about it," Matt prompted softly, so he wouldn't break into her thoughts.

"There's not much to tell, actually. Starla, Madison and I were—"

"Who's Starla?"

"My mother. She didn't want to be called 'Mom' or 'Mama'—said it made her feel old."

"I see," Matt said, and he did . . . more than she realized.

"We were living in Las Vegas at the time, near the casino where she worked as a hostess." Kirby flicked a defiant glance in Matt's direction and paused, as though expecting him to comment.

"Go on," he urged instead.

"Starla was forty-two—a beautiful woman. She had a lot of friends, mostly men, and a lot of clingy, sparkly dresses." Kirby gave him a half smile. "Madison loved those dresses. Starla wouldn't let her touch them, but I let her . . . every time she went away with one of her *clients*." She shrugged. "I guess that was my way of getting even with her for leaving me and Madison alone."

"She did that a lot?"

"Yeah. Sometimes for one night, sometimes for two or three. Once for a week, right before Christmas—the Christmas we got our real tree, as a matter of fact."

"Your mother left a thirteen-year-old in charge of an eight-year-old *for a week?*"

"Yes," Kirby replied. "And we managed quite well. I'd been both mother and sister to Madison for years by then. Of course, the landlady checked in on us every once in a while, which helped keep us on our best behavior."

"And when your mother came home she bought the tree?"

"She didn't buy it. Her fiancé, Clint, did."

"Tell me about him."

Kirby wrinkled her nose in obvious distaste. "What can I say? He was young, early twenties I'd say. Arrogant, egotistical, very flashy—"

"Like Jason?" Matt asked with sudden intuition.

"Exactly like Jason, and that silly Madison was every bit as smitten..." Kirby's words trailed to silence; her eyes widened in shock. "Uh-oh. Do you suppose that's why Jason gets on my nerves so badly? Because he reminds me of Clint?"

"It's quite possible."

Kirby sighed. "Damn. I guess that means I'll have to give him another chance."

"That would be the fair thing to do," Matt agreed, albeit rather reluctantly. He suspected that if she gave Jason another chance, there might not be one left to give Matt Foxx. "Now, about this Clint guy. You said he bought a tree for you girls?"

"Uh-huh, and all the decorations his money could buy. The four of us had a ball putting it up. Oh, I was a little skeptical at first—this wasn't the first 'fiancé' Starla had dragged home, after all—but even I got into the spirit of the thing before it was over. We had a rowdy, wonderful Christmas." She paused, then shook her head. "Too rowdy, I guess. By New Year's Day, Clint grew irritable and restless. And two days later he flew the coop, taking Starla with him."

"How long did she stay gone that time?"

"I haven't seen her since."

Matt caught his breath. At once aching for Kirby and her sister, he blinked back tears of his own.

No wonder she abhorred the Matt Foxx of the tabloids. He undoubtedly reminded her of each and every man who'd crossed her mother's path, just as his publisher reminded her of Clint.

Once again Matt wished he could tell Kirby the truth about his life. How surprised she'd be to find that he rarely dated, and only then so he could have his photo snapped with this or that sweet young thing to keep the gossip lively.

But the truth could not be told, and Jason wasn't the only reason why.

Against all odds, Matt secretly dreamed he'd find a woman willing to accept him unconditionally, bad press and all, no questions asked. Since he realized his expectations might be a little unrealistic, not to mention unfair to the women who crossed his path, he'd always taken the easy way out and kept his Dillon Mathias side a secret.

As for Kirby... Matt quickly decided that if he didn't tell her the truth, he could keep right on fantasizing that she might be *the* woman of his dreams.

"What did you do? Call your grandmother?" Matt asked, finally breaking the heavy silence.

"I didn't even know I had a grandmother."

"Then how did you locate her?"

"I didn't," she replied. "Our landlady did. When the rent came due, she went through all Starla's things looking for cash. She found an old letter with Nana's address on it. A month later Nana came and got us."

"And your grandfather?"

"He died in the Korean War, so I never knew him."

Matt sat without speaking for long moments, amazed that Kirby could tell so tragic a story with so little emotion besides the first few tears she shed.

"Are you bitter?" he asked. "About Starla's deserting you, I mean?"

"Not anymore," Kirby replied. "My mother must have felt as caught and desperate as...well, as ol' Freddie would have if he'd found that trap instead of us."

"You're an amazing woman, Kirby Lee Gibson," Matt murmured, lowering his arm to where it rested lightly on her shoulders.

"First I'm 'compulsive,' then 'nice' and now 'amazing,'" Kirby grumbled with a self-conscious smile. "What's next, I wonder?"

Matt said nothing, suddenly struck silent by another flash of insight: Kirby's sensible life-style undoubtedly resulted from her past. Though simply a survival tactic at one time, it was now a statement against the excesses that could wreck lives.

But what about the bikini panties? he wondered. Didn't they seem to say that Kirby had another side— a frivolous, pink-panty side she kept hidden from the world just as he did his own whimsical, Skeeter Skunk side?

Matt thought so and renewed his determination to get to know Kirby better. Maybe he and Kirby weren't as different as he'd once feared they were. And maybe, just maybe, she was *the one*.

"My goodness, it's after two!" Kirby exclaimed, jolting him from his reverie. "I've got tons of things yet to do today, and you need to be writing."

She got to her feet and extended a hand to tug him to his. When he stood, she guided him to the kitchen and the processor.

"Do I have to?" he moaned, eyeing it with trepidation.

"Yes," she replied, adding, "And try to type *something* this time. Remember, no matter how bad it is, you can always fix it later."

Nodding at her wisdom, Matt sat in the chair and obligingly placed his fingers on the keyboard. He read the words already on the screen, thought for a moment, then began to type.

I'm doing it! I'm actually . . .

. . . doing it! He's doing it! Thrilled, Kirby backed quietly out of the kitchen and into the living room. From there she made a trip to the bathroom.

She groaned when she looked in the mirror over the sink and caught sight of her hair, which hadn't been touched since that morning and now fell in wild disarray about her face and shoulders. After brushing it into some semblance of style, Kirby freshened her makeup. Not once did she consider it odd to bother there in the wilds of Wyoming. There was a man around, after all.

And what a man. So thoughtful. So funny.

So stubborn. Kirby smiled rather sadly, knowing for a certainty she would miss Matt when she left him and her cozy cabin far behind. Closing her eyes, she tried

to imagine herself back in the real world, seated behind a desk or dealing with cost-conscious clients
anxious to streamline production.

Such things didn't matter here on the mountain, and
that was, Kirby decided, most likely the real reason
Matt hadn't been able to complete his book, not any
lack of talent or inspiration.

"Maybe I'd better point that out to my poor, tor-
tured housemate," she murmured aloud with a heartfelt, disgustingly sentimental sigh that told her she
really cared about Matt Foxx. How he'd managed to
get under her skin, she couldn't begin to say.

Shaking her head in wonder, Kirby tiptoed back
through the living room, en route to the porch. By
holding her mouth just so, she managed to open the
front door without so much as a squeak. Pleased with
that accomplishment, she stepped onto the porch and
picked up two of the logs Matt had piled there yesterday.

Yesterday? Kirby wanted to laugh out loud. It
seemed as though she'd known Matt Foxx forever, not
just a matter of hours, a feeling she knew she could
blame on their recent tête-à-tête.

She blushed, remembering how she'd spilled her
guts to him, a virtual stranger. Always a very private
person, Kirby had never felt inclined to tell anyone
about the skeleton in her closet before today.

Why now? she couldn't help but wonder. And why
to this particular man? Bemused, Kirby turned, halting when she spied some mistletoe clustered high in the
bare branches of a tree at the edge of the yard.

What's Christmas without mistletoe? she wondered, abruptly abandoning her logs and stepping right out into the snow, intent on getting her hands on some of that oh-so-traditional greenery.

Kirby gazed up into the limbs, gauging the possibility of climbing the tree. She decided it could be done and grasped a lower limb to lever herself up.

"What are you doing?"

Kirby jumped in surprise at the sound of Matt's voice. The soles of her boots immediately skidded down the tree trunk to the snowy ground. With a huff of irritation, she looked over her shoulder to where Matt stood on the porch.

"What are *you* doing?" she retorted, swiping her aching hands down her jeans.

"Taking a break."

"You've already typed five pages?"

"Five *words* is more like it. I heard you go outside. I wanted to see what you were up to."

He'd *heard* her? Good grief!

Matt jumped off the porch to join her. He tipped his head back, staring up into the tree she'd been trying to climb. "Are you after that mistletoe?"

"Yes."

"You'll never be able to get up there and get it. Besides, you don't need that stuff. I'll let you kiss me any time you want."

"In your dreams, Mr. Foxx." Kirby raised her gaze upward to the mistletoe, took a deep breath and reached for a low branch with hands reddened from the cold.

She pulled herself up and reached for another, and another. Then her feet slipped on the ice-glazed bark, and she fell... right into Matt's waiting arms.

"I seem to be making a habit of this," he commented even as he strode to the porch and set her on her feet. "Stay right here. I'll get the damned mistletoe."

"How?"

"With that ladder your nana's got leaning against the back of the cabin."

At once feeling the fool for not remembering that rickety old ladder, Kirby nodded her agreement. From the shelter of the porch, she waited and watched while Matt risked his neck fetching the mistletoe.

He handed it to her moments later with a gallant bow. "For my lady."

And at once, how she wished that were true.

"Thanks." Embarrassed, Kirby whirled toward the door, her treasure in hand. She nodded toward her forgotten logs. "Get those, will you?"

Matt sighed like an overworked, misunderstood slave, but did as requested. He then trailed her into the house, where he dumped his load.

Relishing the warmth of the cabin, Kirby examined the huge bunch of mistletoe with pleasure and some bewilderment. Now that she had it, what was she going to do with it?

"Want me to hang some in all the doorways?" the ever-helpful Matt Foxx asked.

"No. I want you to go on back to work. Now."

He did... with an injured sniff and obvious reluctance.

Humming "Deck the Halls," Kirby hung one tiny sprig over the front door, then set the rest on the top bunk of Matt's bed. She next dragged the vacuum cleaner from the closet to clean up under the tree so she could bunch a white sheet around the trunk of it to serve as a skirt.

She flipped it on and managed two swipes with the nozzle before Matt stepped into her path. "Want some help?" he yelled over the roar.

Kirby held on to her patience with difficulty. "No, Matt."

"Then I'll dust."

"No, Matt."

"Should I go out and start up our vehicles to give their batteries a charge?"

"I have a brand-new one. It should be fine."

"I've got it! The laundry—"

"Matt!" she exploded, at the end of her rope.

"What?"

"Get to work!"

As before, he did but he grumbled and growled with every step back to the kitchen.

Thoroughly disgusted with her, with himself and with life in general, Matt sat down in front of the word processor for the third time that day. Impatiently he waited for the new idea, the surge of inspiration that would finally topple the writer's block threatening his reputation and his livelihood.

He squeezed his eyes shut, hoping that when he opened them again he would see something on that screen to trigger his imagination and therefore his enthusiasm.

"Come on Ross, ol' buddy," he muttered, flexing his fingers in his eagerness to make that old magic again. "Do something brave. Do something heroic. Hell, do *anything!*"

But Ross steadfastly ignored him, and there was no new idea, no surge of inspiration, no anything.

Abruptly the last remnant of Matt's waning enthusiasm vanished, taking with it his control.

Furious with himself, Matt snatched up his ever-present coffee mug and threw it against the wall, where it shattered into a million pieces.

Chapter Six

Matt winced at the sound, but felt no real remorse. In fact, he half wished for something else to hurl.

"What was that?" Kirby demanded from the doorway behind him.

"That was the sound of my writing career smashing to smithereens." Matt propped his elbows on the table and buried his face in his hands, groaning. "Why, oh why did I ever agree to write this asinine book?"

"You tell me," Kirby said, walking over to perch on the edge of the table near the keyboard.

"Damned if I know." Matt raised his weary head and met her gaze square on. "All I can tell you is that I'm sick of assassination, sick of intrigue and sick of Ross Elliot!"

This is even more serious than I imagined, Kirby thought, eyeing him with growing alarm. Clearly it was time for desperate measures. "Yesterday you said you wanted to bounce around a plot idea. How about now...?"

"If I had a plot idea I'd *use* it, not bounce it around," Matt snapped.

"There's no reason to get huffy," Kirby replied in what she considered a saintly show of patience. "I'm only trying to help. Let me see your outline. Maybe I'll have a brainstorm."

"What outline? I sell and write from a one-page premise."

Kirby's jaw dropped. Her eyes rounded in astonishment. "You're teasing. Tell me you're teasing."

"I sell and write from a one-page premise," Matt repeated, somewhat defensively adding, "I always have."

"But that's so... so... *disorganized.*"

"It's worked fine for me until now."

"Which is surely a bigger miracle than the one on Thirty-fourth Street *or* Gibson Ridge. Outlining is a tried-and-true writing technique, Matt. I honestly believe that you'll be able to finish your book if you stop right now and make one."

"But I don't know the first thing about them."

"That's okay. Outlines are a specialty of mine." She hopped off the table. "Come on. Let's work in the living room. It's warmer in there." She headed to the door, pausing to look back at Matt, who hadn't moved a muscle to follow. "You'd rather do it in here?"

"I'd rather not do it at all," he said. "I've written all my other books without one. I can write this book, too."

"But Matt—"

"I'm not wasting my time on an outline and that's final!"

"Fine, then. Waste your time pouting instead!" With that, Kirby stomped from the kitchen, leaving him alone with his bad temper.

For the next hour Matt passed the time alternately staring at the computer monitor and out the window. His temper died a natural death as the minutes slowly ticked away. Finally, in utter desperation, he scooted back his chair and walked to the living room door, as near ready to choke down some humble pie as he'd ever been.

He peeked his head inside the room and found Kirby sitting on the couch. He could see she held a small wooden embroidery hoop and was stitching on the white cloth stretched over it.

From where he stood, she appeared to be quite calm and content. Encouraged, Matt squared his shoulders and walked on into the room. Silently he sat beside her on the couch.

She never so much as glanced his way.

Matt noted that she had put on a pair of glasses and tied her hair back with a ribbon, probably to keep it out of her face while she sewed. In spite of her gorgeous looks, she looked rather like a schoolmarm, he thought. The kind who just loved to rap a wooden ruler across the knuckles of rebellious students.

"I've, uh, decided to give your idea a try," he blurted, a little disconcerted by his vivid mental imagery. "I'm going to make an outline of the rest of the book."

"You won't regret it," she said, methodically dipping her needle in and out of the fabric she held.

"I was kind of hoping you'd help."

Kirby set her work in her lap. She took off her glasses and raised her gaze to meet his. "I'm busy right now."

"Okay. Later."

"I'm busy then, too."

Matt swallowed hard and tried again. "Look, Kirby. I know you want an apology from me, and Lord knows I just might owe you one, but it's hard for me to say I'm sorry."

"It's hard for you to say *what?*"

"I'm sorry."

Kirby flashed a brilliant smile. "Apology accepted!" she exclaimed, delivering a stinging slap of victory to his denimed thigh. She leaned up and retrieved a pad of paper and a pencil from behind her back. "Have a seat. We've got work to do."

And work they did. At Kirby's prompting, Matt verbalized a summary of what had transpired thus far in his book. When she asked what was going to happen next, he told her what he originally had in mind.

Kirby grimaced.

"You don't like it?" Matt asked.

"Well... No."

"My publisher did."

"Which probably explains why I don't," she retorted. "But hey, it's your book. Write it the way you want to."

"Believe me. I would if I could."

"Why do you suppose you can't?" Kirby asked, drawing up one knee and resting her chin on it.

She looked so wide-eyed, so wondering. It was all Matt could do not to snatch up a sprig of that mistletoe, which she'd probably hidden from him, and hold it over her head so he'd have an excuse to kiss her.

He immediately decided it was probably best he didn't have so handy an excuse. If he got lucky and one kiss led to another, he would definitely never finish his book.

"I once heard that if you get stuck on what you're writing, you should check to see if everyone is in character."

"And are they?" Kirby asked.

"Well, my hero is for sure." Matt frowned, mentally replaying the scenes over which he'd labored the past few months. "And so is his archrival."

"What about your heroine?"

"Who cares about her? She's just there to make Ross look good."

"And that, if you ask me, is your problem," Kirby announced. "Ross never sleeps alone. But when it comes to his work, he flies solo. Frankly I think that's a crock."

"Would you care to expound on that?"

"Gladly," she replied, and proceeded to...with care to choose her words wisely. This was the opportunity for which Kirby had waited. She did not intend to blow it now. "What is your favorite book in the world?"

Without hesitation, Matt named a political thriller Kirby knew had been on the bestseller lists for weeks.

"I meant to read that, but never did," she told him. "I saw the movie, though. Was it like the book?"

"Very close."

"Hmm. As I recall, the heroine played a pivotal role in the scheme of things. Am I right?"

"Yes," Matt admitted.

"In fact, I believe she was the one who broke into the embassy and found the crucial tapes—the ones that implicated the ambassador."

"I believe so, yes."

"And weren't she and the hero very much in love?"

Matt huffed in obvious impatience. "I know what you're getting at and I admit that books without some measure of romance aren't as popular. That's why I put so many love scenes in mine."

"Love scenes! You call those love scenes?"

Kirby leapt to her feet and walked over to the fireplace, where she rested her hands on the edge of the mantel and her forehead on her hands. She gazed into the blazing logs without seeing them, surprisingly distressed that Matt didn't seem to know the difference between love and lust.

Somehow, in spite of everything she'd read about him, she had secretly hoped...

"What do *you* call them?" he asked softly from right beside her. He propped an elbow on the mantel.

"Sex scenes. Ross uses women, Matt. *Uses them.* He gives a little pleasure, gets a lot and then vanishes into the night. I, for one, find that insulting. This is the nineties. Women are liberated—just like that little old lady you tried to help across the street. We have brains. We hold down jobs. We earn money. *We buy books*. We deserve a little respect.''

Matt stood in silence for a moment, obviously stunned, then shook his head. ''Are you actually suggesting that Lola LaMay help Ross on his case.''

''That's exactly what I'm suggesting. Just think what a plot twist that would be! Your fans would love it.''

''I'm not so sure....'' Matt murmured, but Kirby could almost see the wheels of conjecture beginning to turn inside his head. Clearly lost in thought, Matt walked back to the couch and sat down. Kirby followed and situated herself beside him, her gaze never leaving his face.

''So what do you think?'' she prompted after he didn't speak for several long minutes.

He made no reply, just got to his feet and headed toward the kitchen.

''Matt...?''

He stopped, glanced her way with glazed eyes, then vanished through the door. Kirby heard the chair being scooted back. Heard the click of the keyboard as Matt began to type...furiously.

She jumped up and pirouetted her jubilation, her arms outflung to hug the room, the cabin, the mountain, the world.

''Yes!'' she exclaimed. ''Ye-e-e-s!''

* * *

Kirby glanced at her watch. Five o'clock. Not quite dinnertime, but close enough since she'd only eaten a few bites of popcorn for lunch and was darned hungry. Did she dare disturb Matt by going to the kitchen?

She thought not and, smiling at the fact that Matt had actually been working for over an hour, Kirby put away her counted cross-stitch and reached for one of her magazines. Some of them were quite old, and not for the first time Kirby wondered why she subscribed to so many when she never had time to read.

Then she remembered the towheaded kid who'd come to the door selling them. He'd as good as begged her to buy, and softhearted woman that she was, Kirby had cooperated.

"This heart of mine is going to get me into serious trouble someday," she muttered even as she acknowledged that it probably already had.

Probably? There was no probably about it. In the short time she'd known Matt, he'd somehow managed to challenge each and every one of her prejudices against him. Now she wasn't sure what to believe. Was he the playboy of the tabloids? Or had the press maligned him?

Kirby thought back to the times when she had questioned Matt about his reputation. He always skirted the issue and never admitted to anything. Why? she now wondered.

It seemed to her that if he were proud of his image, he would brag on it. On the other hand, if he wasn't proud, why didn't he defend his honor?

Very confused, Kirby began to flip absently through her magazine. Suddenly, from page fifteen a very dashing Matt Foxx smiled up at her. He wore a tux, a brunette and a redhead.

Kirby's soft heart immediately hardened.

She glared at the photo, obviously snapped at one of the night spots that celebrities such as Matt frequented. So much for the tabloids maligning Matt. Photographs did not lie, even if reporters sometimes did.

Disgusted, perhaps a little jealous of Matt's busty glamour girls, Kirby looked ahead to the time when she would tell him goodbye. She imagined herself back in Cheyenne again and wondered how she would feel when she saw his picture on the jacket of his book when it finally hit the shelves.

Relief that she wasn't just another notch on his bedpost? Or regret that they never shared more than insults and a few confidences?

Kirby laughed aloud at that craziness and got to her feet, heading for the kitchen and food without further ado. If she ever thought of Matt once she got back to Cheyenne—and Kirby wasn't planning to—she would congratulate herself on a job well done.

Nothing more.

On tiptoe, Kirby entered the kitchen. Matt never stopped typing. Pleased at his concentration—clearly he was on a creative roll—she made her way to the refrigerator and took from it a jug of apple cider.

Kirby measured some into a saucepan and set it on a burner of the stove. After turning up the heat, she added a few cinnamon candies to spice it up, then, because her nana raised her right, turned to Matt.

"Would you like a mug of hot apple cider?" she asked.

He didn't so much as glance her way.

"All right, then. How about a peanut-butter-and-honey sandwich?"

Still no response.

Kirby almost went over to tap on Matt's shoulder to get his attention, but caught herself. Obviously he "burned" with one of those ideas he'd once told her about. Since this is what they'd both prayed for, she'd do well to leave him to it. He could always eat later.

Besides, having him in the kitchen beat the heck out of having him underfoot.

Minutes later, Kirby took her steaming mug and her sandwich back to the living room. Matt said nothing when she slipped past him, just pushed his hair back out of his eyes and typed on.

The evening dragged by. Outside, snow fell silently and without ceasing. Inside, the fire crackled and popped. Kirby made herself stay in the living room, which wasn't nearly so cozy now that Matt wasn't there with her.

She felt alternately lonely and abandoned, foolish feelings she despised. Nine o'clock came and went without so much as a peep out of Matt. Ten o'clock followed, then eleven, and, an eternity after that, midnight.

Kirby picked up the last unread magazine, fully intending to read it, then tossed it back down.

"This is ridiculous," she said, getting to her feet. She walked to her bathroom, took a shower and went to bed.

And this night she slept.

When Kirby opened her eyes Sunday morning, her watch said seven o'clock. She peeked out the window for a weather check—snow again—then dressed in corduroy pants and a jade green sweater Madison had given her last Christmas.

Kirby took a moment to miss her little sister and wonder what mischief she was up to in Vermont. Most likely she was having brunch with Jason's family—it was midmorning there—or perhaps she was on her way to a mall to do some last-minute shopping, also with Jason's family.

Meanwhile, big sister Kirby whiled away the hours twiddling her thumbs in the wilds of Wyoming....

"Shame on you," Kirby scolded herself.

Isn't that exactly what she'd come here for? But of course it was. Unfortunately the two people with whom she had planned to share the cabin and her holiday were sadly absent. Never mind that they'd asked her to come along with them to Vermont, an invitation stubborn pride would not let her accept.

What mattered was that she now found herself holed up with the headliner of America's trashiest tabloids.

What's worse, he'd slipped over the edge of reality and into a fantasy world of spies, secrets and high-tech weaponry.

On that thought, Kirby made her way to the living room to wake her housemate so he could get back to work. But he was already up... or had he ever been down?

Kirby frowned at Matt's bunk, which looked exactly as rumpled as it had yesterday. Seriously doubting that he'd even slept there, she hurried to the kitchen, stopping short in the door when she spied Matt sitting in exactly the same position as the last time she saw him and wearing the same clothes.

Horrified that he would work so many hours without sleep or food, Kirby started forward to scold him, but didn't when she spied a plate and a glass in the sink.

Obviously he'd eaten at some point. But had he slept?

"Matt?"

"Hmm?" His fingers never ceased typing.

"Where did you sleep last night?"

"Couch. Bunk's too damned short."

Kirby exhaled her pent-up breath. At least he'd stopped writing long enough to sleep and eat. That showed a certain amount of sanity. And he knew she was in the room... another plus. "Want some breakfast?"

"Uh-uh."

Kirby stared at him a moment in fascination. Talk about dedication... Impressed in spite of herself, she went about her own business of preparing a light meal. Shortly after found her sitting alone in the living room eating it.

After breakfast Kirby picked up her sewing. She worked halfheartedly on it until eight-thirty, at which time she tossed down the hoop and restlessly paced the room.

She peeked out to see if the snow had stopped—it had—then threw another log on the fire. That accomplished, Kirby walked back to the couch, where she managed to sit for five long minutes before she leapt to her feet and headed to the kitchen, seeking of all things, a snack.

Matt hadn't moved a muscle other than the ones in his fingers.

Humming "Have Yourself a Merry Little Christmas" just a little too loudly, Kirby dug through the refrigerator for something to eat. Nothing appealed to her, probably because she'd consumed breakfast barely an hour ago.

Eventually Kirby decided on one of the caffeine-free diet colas she'd brought to the cabin. She took out one of Matt's root beers, as well, and after popping the top, set it on the table right next to the keyboard.

Without shifting his gaze from the computer screen, Matt picked up the can and drank down the whole twelve ounces in one long gulp. Then he set it down, brushed his hair out of his eyes and began to type again.

Somewhat encouraged by that show of normalcy, Kirby asked once again, if he wanted something to eat . . . a sandwich, maybe, or some hot soup.

Matt grunted what was most likely meant to be a no.

Kirby frowned, as reluctant to return to the prison cell she'd once called a living room as she was worried about her hardworking housemate.

How long could he sit in that awful chair at a stretch? she wondered. Didn't he know how important it was to get up and exercise his muscles every now and then?

Honestly concerned for him, she impulsively blurted an offer to cut his hair so he could see to type. It wouldn't take long, and the short break could only do him good.

Matt only grunted again, this one a definite no.

Though tempted to argue, Kirby didn't. He was, after all, a grown man who could take care of himself. And she was a grown woman who had better things to do than sit around and pout because he didn't have time to entertain her.

So why this depression, this boredom, this restlessness? Was she just like her mother, who couldn't function without a man by her side?

Appalled at the very idea, Kirby decided to get out of the cabin for a while so she wouldn't gravitate to the kitchen and disturb Matt again. After telling him where she was going—he didn't even bother to grunt this time—she put on her coat, hat and gloves. Snatching up her camera and two extra rolls of film, Kirby dashed outdoors.

The brisk winter wind quickly cleared the cobwebs from Kirby's muddled mind, just as she'd hoped it would. Determined to ignore any last lingering worries about Matt, she joyfully explored the familiar woods, taking photographs of an especially gorgeous tree, a snowshoe hare and a mountain chickadee. She watched for Freddie Fox, hoping to get one of him, too, but had no luck.

Kirby lost track of time as she explored her old stamping grounds, but never her sense of direction. Light snow began to fall around four-thirty that afternoon. Glorying in it, she took another dozen photos and then, urged homeward by her growling tummy, Kirby finally headed back to shelter just before six o'clock.

At the edge of the clearing, she spied several pinecones that had somehow withstood the elements and still clung to the branches of a ponderosa pine. At once picturing how Christmasy those cones would look in one of her nana's handmade baskets, Kirby stopped to collect them.

She unbuttoned her jacket and lifted up the hem of her sweater to form a pouch. One by one she tossed the cones into it until she had an even dozen, more than enough to fill the particular basket she had in mind.

Kirby then resumed her trek to the cabin, noting with surprise that the charcoal gray sky had darkened to ebony. But the windows at the back of the cabin glowed a welcome up ahead, and replete with the day's pleasures she gladly approached.

The moment Kirby rounded the corner of the cabin, she halted in surprise at the sight of Matt, standing on the lighted porch in a getup befitting the leader of an Alaskan expedition—heavy coat, stocking cap, boots, gloves, flashlight....

"Where are you going?" she asked, closing the remaining distance between them.

Matt whirled at the sound of her voice, then leapt off the porch to engulf Kirby in a bear hug that poked the prickly pinecones right through the bulky knit of her sweater into her ribs.

"Ow!" she exclaimed, squirming for freedom.

Matt released her reluctantly and only because she made such a fuss.

"Where the hell have you been?" he demanded.

"Don't curse at me!"

"I'm not, dammit!" Matt heard his expletive echo through the woods and winced. "Sorry."

"I believe you're getting better at that," Kirby commented, as though the two of them chatted over tea and crumpets. She walked to the porch and pried pinecone after pinecone from her sweater, laying them in a neat row before her. Only when she'd finished did she look Matt's way again. "Now then, what did you ask me?"

Matt locked his hands behind his back to keep from wringing her pretty little neck. "Where...have... you...been?" he repeated, enunciating each word with care.

"Exploring. Why?"

"Why?" Matt was beside her again in two long strides. Clasping her shoulders, he turned her to face him. "Because I've been worried sick about you, that's why."

"But I told you I was going out," she reminded him, twisting free.

"At eight forty-two this morning," he retorted. "That was almost nine hours ago."

"You actually noticed?" She sounded surprised.

Matt nearly choked.

Kirby actually thought he wouldn't notice that she no longer sashayed past his chair every five minutes? Matt Foxx, who'd relied on willpower he didn't know he possessed to keep his seat when she asked him to drink and dine with her? Matt Foxx, who would've traded his computer *and* his career for that haircut she volunteered to give him?

Amazing. And equally amazing, not to mention darned encouraging, was the fact that she actually seemed a little *put out* by his dedication to duty, which wasn't that at all, but a sincere fear that a coffee break would rock or capsize his creative boat.

"I noticed," he told her, somehow not laughing at that vast understatement. In truth, he'd yelled himself hoarse for her, made like a bloodhound and finally resorted to the antique ham radio stuck way back on a dusty shelf in the kitchen.

He'd actually reached someone, too—an old codger named Walter, who'd asked a lot of nosy questions and offered no help at all.

All these frantic attempts to locate Kirby, coupled with this gut relief at her appearance could only mean one thing, Matt abruptly realized.

If he wasn't in love already, he didn't have far to fall. Kirby was *the one*. But did she want to be?

"You never told me where you're going," the woman in question said at that moment. Her bright eyes swept him from head to toe in open curiosity.

"Nowhere...now. I *was* going to look for you again."

"Again?"

"I combed the immediate area for you hours ago. The snow had covered your tracks, though."

"Then how did you expect to find me in the dark?" He could see she struggled not to smile, and bristled in indignation.

"What else could I do? Leave you out here to freeze to death?"

At once Kirby sobered. "You really were worried about me." Her eyes rounded in wonder.

"Of course I was."

Women! Hadn't she guessed how he felt about her by now? Or did she think he'd risk his neck in the wild woods of Wyoming for any woman? Obviously it was time to make a serious move—one that even a slow learner such as Kirby could interpret.

Thank goodness he knew how his book was going to end now and had four critical chapters plus some rediscovered self-confidence under his belt. He could devote every day—and night—to Kirby's seduction.

"Then I owe *you* an apology," Kirby said. "I'm sorry I stayed out so long today, Matt. It was very inconsiderate of me, and I'll do anything to make it up to you."

"Even stand under that mistletoe you put over the front door this morning?" he asked, half expecting to get his face slapped for his impudence.

To his surprise, Kirby climbed the stairs to the porch and stepped inside the cabin, stopping right under the sprig he'd spotted on one of his many trips outside that evening.

She turned and smiled at him. "I'm waiting...."

Chapter Seven

Not for long. With a leap and a bound, Matt joined Kirby under the mistletoe and wrapped his arms around her in an enthusiastic hug that was one part relief and nine parts desire.

She returned his embrace full measure, raising up on tiptoe to touch her lips to his in a chaste kiss Matt suspected was nine parts apology and only one part desire. For that reason, he relished the sweet, sweet contact and decided then and there to decorate each and every door-facing in the cabin with a sprig of that mistletoe—if he could locate it, that is. He certainly didn't want to climb up into the old tree again.

When Kirby ended the kiss mere moments later, Matt released her with reluctance. To his surprise, she didn't release him. Instead, she clung, whispering, "Welcome back to the real world. I missed you."

She'd missed him? Now that was luck he didn't deserve.

At once Matt rejoiced that he hadn't yet told Kirby the truth about his alter ego. In his opinion, missing someone was the first step toward loving them. And if a woman of her background could actually fall in love with a world-famous "womanizer" such as Matt Foxx, her love could only be true.

Matt wanted that unconditional love. And only when he had it would he spill his guts to her... Jason or no.

"Enough to cook tonight even though it's probably my turn?" he teased, suddenly lighthearted.

"If it's that or eat breakfast for dinner again, then yes, I'll be the cook." She let go of him and turned, starting toward the kitchen, but stopped and faced him once more. "Are you going back to work after you eat?"

"I should. Why?"

"Just wondering," she replied. She made it all the way to the door, then halted once more. "What are you hungry for?"

You. Matt cleared his throat and tried to get his wayward thoughts in line. "Hot dogs? I have all the makings."

Kirby grimaced. "Are you sure?"

"Uh-huh. And on the side, I want baked beans. There's a can in the pantry."

"I see."

"And french fries would be good."

"All right. Is that all?"

"Yes, except for the chili, of course. I have a can of that somewhere, too." He noted her disapproving expression. "You can't have hot dogs without chili."

Kirby heaved a sigh. "Then by all means, let's have chili. Now, is *that* all?"

"That's all," he replied. "And should be enough to keep you busy until I shower and shave—"

"You're going to shave again?" Kirby interjected.

"Yes." Matt walked to his suitcase, which lay open on the top bunk bed, and extracted a change of clothes from it. Beside the suitcase he spied the bunch of slightly wilted mistletoe he thought Kirby had hidden. With a grin of triumph and a solid excuse for stealing another kiss or three, he headed for the shower.

Kirby got straight to work in the kitchen. Having cooked hot dogs only a couple of times in her adult life—she'd always considered their ingredients highly questionable—Kirby saved preparation of those for last. Instead, she heated the beans and fried the potatoes.

Just as she finished up that part of the meal, Matt strolled into the kitchen—fully dressed, freshly shaved and sexy as all get-out. Willingly he joined a thoroughly distracted Kirby at the stove, where he coached her in the fine art of building a hot dog. He heated the weiners, placed them on buns and proceeded to pile on mustard, catsup, relish, chili, onions and cheese.

Kirby, whose gaze rested on the animated chef more often than his concoction, eyed the finished product with considerable alarm when he finally handed it to her. Matt then led the way to the living room, where they consumed the surprisingly delicious, if not exactly nutritious, meal.

Little was said until their appetites waned. Then Matt talked nonstop, sharing the plot twist he'd worked into his story. Basking in his undivided attention, Kirby listened intently.

"Perfect," she told him when he finished his narrative. "Your fans are going to love it."

"You know, I think you're right." He smiled. "I'm really grateful for your help on this book, Kirby. In fact, I believe I'll dedicate it to you."

"Don't be silly. That's an honor reserved for family or someone you love."

"There's no one in this world I'd rather choose," Matt told her. "No one." His blue eyes glowed. His smile warmed her.

"Thank you," she whispered, touched nearly to tears. Her misty gaze dropped to his mouth, and suddenly her lips ached to be pressed to his again.

And that wasn't the only body part clamoring for attention. Gradually Kirby became aware of the fact that there were other parts—secret, private parts—that craved close contact with Matt. At once her heart thudded against her rib cage.

Desperately in need of breathing space, Kirby scrambled to her feet. "I-I'll do the dishes. I'm sure you're anxious to get back to work...."

"I was kind of hoping you'd give me a haircut first." Matt ran his fingers through still-damp tresses. "This stuff is driving me nuts."

"Well, I..." Kirby swallowed hard. This afternoon cutting Matt's hair had seemed like a good idea.

Now it didn't. In fact, the mere thought gave her a fluttery feeling deep in the pit of her stomach. Kirby struggled for composure, somehow managing a weak smile. It wouldn't do to reveal the muddled state of her usually sensible head. It wouldn't do at all. "Sure," she said with a deliberately casual shrug. "Why not?"

"Do I need to wet it again?" He leaned forward so she could touch that golden brown mane. Kirby only pretended to.

"Oh, yes." Anything to delay the inevitable.

While Matt ducked his head under the kitchen faucet, Kirby retreated to the bedroom in search of Nana's sewing box and scissors. She felt a twinge of guilt when she reached for them and smiled when she realized the reason—years of warnings not to cut anything except fabric with those precious, razor-sharp shears.

Kirby's lighter mood prevailed until she walked back into the living room and spied Matt, who'd set a kitchen chair in the middle of the floor. He'd shed his T-shirt, most likely to keep it dry and free of hair. That bare chest, to which she had a documented vulnerability, in combination with his smooth jawline were a double whammy and almost too much for Kirby to handle.

To make matters worse, the droplets of water dotting his shoulders caught the glow of the fire and glistened topaz golden against his tanned skin. Kirby feasted on the sight and decided she wouldn't be surprised to see Matt's photo in another magazine someday, not as a headliner, but in an ad ... for a man's cologne with a name such as "Lust" or maybe "Sin."

"Want me to spread some newspapers on the floor?" Matt asked.

With a guilty start, Kirby abandoned her fantasy. "I'll sweep up what doesn't stick to your towel," she said, reaching out for the towel and comb Matt held.

He handed them to her and sat down, obviously at ease.

A nervous wreck herself—and not because she didn't think she'd do a good job—Kirby draped the towel over his wide shoulders, then assessed his hair—thick, honey colored and begging to be touched.

She reached to do exactly that but hesitated, momentarily overwhelmed by the sheer masculinity—and proximity—of him.

One-two-three-go! she silently coached, this time actually putting her fingers to his hair, which was every bit as thick as it looked and unexpectedly silky. Kirby barely kept her feet on the ground as a wave of intense desire washed over her. She gulped audibly and began to comb. "How do you want this, anyway?"

"Short," Matt told her.

With hands that trembled, Kirby pulled up and carefully snipped section after section of hair. As she worked, her fingers brushed against his forehead, his ears and finally his neck—a new, remarkably sensual experience that left her weak as a kitten and wild as the blue norther blowing outside.

"All done," Kirby announced with considerable relief a short time later. Much more of this, and he might not have to worry about sleeping on that narrow couch or that too-short bunk tonight. He would surely find himself snug and warm in a big iron bed...along with the wanton housemate who'd dragged him there.

Not for the first time ruing the pride that had brought her to this mountain, Kirby brushed the loose hair from his head and shoulders and carefully removed the towel.

"Thanks so much," Matt said, turning his head to look back at her. "I—ow!" He rubbed a hand over the back of his neck.

"What's wrong?" Kirby asked.

"I have a crick right here." He pointed to an area just to the left of his spine.

"Well, that's no wonder," she responded, momentarily distracted from her bedroom thoughts. With her fingertips, she gently probed the spot he'd indicated. "Why, you're tense as a coiled spring. I knew all that typing without a break couldn't be good for you."

Honestly concerned, Kirby began to knead those taut muscles. Matt dropped his head forward, giving her better access to his muscled neck.

She worked in silence, massaging the tension away. His skin felt hot to the touch, and some of that heat found its way to Kirby. At once on fire for him, she threw caution to that blue norther and leaned down to touch her lips to the flesh just below his earlobe.

Matt tensed, then reached back. With a firm tug, he guided Kirby to the front of the chair and pulled her right down onto his lap.

"What are you doing?" she gasped, so surprised that she hadn't the wits to resist.

"A man can only stand so much," Matt said, crushing her to him. "*That* was my limit."

"So what happens now?" Kirby asked rather breathlessly, glorying in the thud of his heart against her splayed fingers, the warmth of his breath against her cheek.

"This." Matt covered her lips with his in a hungry kiss that threatened to consume her.

Kirby melted to him and, as ravenous as Matt, gave herself freely to the passion of his kiss. His tongue teased her lips for entry—an intimacy she'd never allowed any man. Kirby responded with abandon, opening her mouth to his exploration and shivering when he probed and tasted.

His husky moan matched hers. Kirby sagged against him, resting her forehead on his chin.

Abruptly Matt got to his feet, nearly dumping Kirby before he swept her into his arms and strode over to the fireplace. He set her on the floor in front of it, then dropped down to lie facing her, his elbow on the floor, his head propped in his hand.

Without hesitation or heed to the alarms sounding in her oh-so-sensible head, Kirby stretched out the long length of him. She cuddled close, tucking her head under Matt's chin. He held her tightly with his free arm.

Several silent moments passed before either moved. Kirby cherished the peace and something else she couldn't put a name to, probably because she'd never experienced it before: a sense of security, of homecoming.

"I'll Be Home for Christmas," that old holiday song, came to mind. At once Kirby knew what the songwriter tried to say. "Home" was more than four walls and a roof. Home was a state of mind. And for the first time in her life, Kirby believed she'd found it.

Awed by this apparent miracle—the second in as many days—she gazed up at Matt, who was not at all the sort of man she'd expected or even imagined could give her such a sense of belonging. Maybe there's more to him than meets the eye, she thought. Maybe her intuition guided her tonight and not his notorious sexual skill.

At that moment Matt reached to retrieve a throw pillow from the nearby couch. He settled his head back on it, then shifted slightly so that Kirby lay half on top of him. Caught up in her hopeful fantasies of hearth and home, she rested her forearms on his chest and seriously studied his handsome face for a possible clue to the mystery of Matt Foxx.

Matt smiled at her, then raised his head for a kiss she willingly gave. He moved his hands over her back and then under her sweater, lightly tracing her spine with his fingertips. Everywhere he touched she tingled, and Kirby did not protest when his fingers found the clasp of her bra and unfastened it, or when he suddenly rolled her over on her back and pushed her sweater and lacy pink bra up to her chin.

His breathing dangerously ragged, Matt molded the fullness of one breast with his hand. He flicked his tongue over the rosy tip, which instantly hardened in desire the likes of which Kirby had never known before.

"Oh, my," she gasped.

"Did I hurt you?" Matt raised his gaze, if not his mouth.

"Oh, no," she whispered.

He grinned and, obviously taking Kirby's quick reply as permission to proceed, trailed his lips from that
breast to the other, and then kissed his way down her
stomach.

Kirby squirmed with pleasure and arched against
him, oblivious to the wailing wind and the sleet
dancing against the windowpanes. All that mattered
was the magic of the moment.

Surely not just any man could make her feel this
way. Matt had to be her destiny...had to be. And since
he was, it was all right to take whatever he gave and to
give whatever he asked.

For that reason she raised no protest when Matt
unfastened the button on her jeans and lowered the
zipper, tooth...by...tooth. Just as Matt accomplished his mission and slipped a hand inside to caress
the flesh below her navel and above her bikini panties, Kirby heard—unbelievably—the roar of an engine outside.

Before she could react, Matt leapt to his feet, and
peered out the window.

He saw—unbelievably—headlights, bobbing as the
vehicle to which they were attached lurched its way
through the ice-dipped trees to the cabin.

"Damn!" Matt exploded. Why, after two months
without a visitor, did someone have to show up *now?*
He'd been so close to winning Kirby, a victory he believed would reveal the state of her heart. And when
she did, he'd reveal the state of his own heart and
gladly share the secret of his dual careers.

"Who is it?" Kirby asked from just behind, shoving his shirt into his hands. Matt didn't have to look back to know she'd put her clothes back in order. He quickly pulled his shirt over his head.

"Beats the heck out of me." He stepped back so she could look out at their intruder.

"Why, it's Walter!" Kirby exclaimed, reaching to open the door. She stepped out on the lighted porch and waved. Matt, who wasn't quite in control of his emotions or his love-tensed body, didn't follow past the door. Instead, he stuck his head out and sucked in several chilly breaths to cool his overheated libido.

From the doorway, he watched the truck pull to a stop, watched Kirby bound right out into the wind-blown sheet of snow and straight into the embrace of the grizzliest old man Matt had ever seen.

All of five foot two or maybe five-three, he wore a cowboy hat, a denim jacket with sheepskin collar and jeans tucked into tall boots.

Even from his several-feet-away vantage point, Matt spotted a twinkle in the old man's eye, and he noted with awe his bushy white beard.

Matt decided that if this Walter fellow had a hundred or so more pounds on his wiry frame, he could pass as Santa Claus. As it was, he resembled one of the elves—and a half-starved one at that.

"Let's get under cover," Kirby said to their guest. With a sigh of resignation, Matt stepped out and waited until the two of them dashed onto the porch. "Matt, this is Walter Williams, a friend of my grandmother's and mine. Walter, Matt Foxx, my, um, *guest*." Kirby blushed when she said that, and Matt cringed, knowing full well what the old man must be thinking.

Walter took the hand Matt automatically extended and shook it. His steady gaze never wavered, an assessment the writer found quite disconcerting. "It was you I talked to on the radio?"

Matt nodded in reply to Walter's question. "And you were right. Kirby did find her way back."

Walter nodded. "Figured she would, but I came by to check, all the same."

Matt said nothing, guessing that wasn't the only reason for the surprise visit.

"Well, now that you're here, you've got to stay for a while," Kirby interjected with a quick glance at Matt and a self-conscious laugh. "I haven't seen you since Nana's funeral and I want to hear all the latest." With that, she slipped her hand in Walter's and led him to the warmth indoors.

Matt followed more slowly, trying to decipher Kirby's apparent eagerness to ask Walter inside. Did she really want to hear "all the latest," or had another motive prompted Walter's invitation?

Did she already regret what had nearly happened? Was her sensible head overruling the not-so-sensible heart he suspected she had?

"Sit down. I'll make some hot chocolate," Kirby told Walter.

"Never touch the stuff," he drawled.

"How about coffee," Matt said. "Would you drink a cup of that?"

Walter gave him another long look, then sat down on the couch and crossed his arms over his chest as though he might be there for the duration. "I take mine black."

Matt headed to the kitchen. Minutes later he served the first of the several cups of coffee Walter consumed during his three-hour visit.

The first half hour of that visit passed rather slowly for Matt. He listened to this and that piece of news about this and that area resident, none of whom he knew or cared anything about.

Then Walter began to reminisce about past Christmases, most of them shared with Kirby's nana. Gradually Matt came to realize that Walter was an old beau of that woman's and could be a valuable source of trivia about her eldest granddaughter.

So the next two hours were spent asking questions about said granddaughter and enjoying some witty, marvelously personal anecdotes.

More than once an obviously embarrassed Kirby tried to redirect Walter's flow of words with a question about the country store he apparently owned or his four children by a long-deceased wife. Walter answered each question with a monosyllabic reply, then went right back to Matt's favorite topic of conversation: Kirby Lee Gibson.

Matt learned that she used to hike to the store via a three-mile-long shortcut through the woods every Saturday morning to do the grocery shopping for her nana, who didn't have a car. Walter said Kirby never missed a Saturday in the summer months and always arrived at ten-thirty on the dot.

Matt never doubted that for a moment.

Walter also said that during the winter months, he made deliveries and was rewarded for his efforts by lunch, usually cooked by a teenage Kirby and always something less than palatable, but very "good" for him.

He smiled when he mentioned that, brown eyes twinkling with the unmistakable pleasure of an old and cherished memory. Having sampled a similarly flavored, equally nutritious meal, Matt never doubted that story, either.

By the time Matt's watch said ten-thirty, he'd learned that Kirby had excelled in all her classes in junior high and high school and organized a homework club to help her less-than-brilliant friends. He also learned that she had doubled her grandmother's sewing business by advertising and organization, and that she helped Walter set up a foolproof billing system and collect on some old debts.

Clearly Walter loved "the girlie," as he called Kirby. And for that reason, Matt graciously forgave him for dropping in and for the last half hour of conversation, which consisted of pointed questions regarding Matt's profession, marital status and reasons for spending his holiday in the wilds of Wyoming.

When Walter finally got to his feet and shuffled to the door, Matt almost hated to see him go. Nonetheless, he still heaved a sigh of relief when the old man got into his truck, turned it and headed back through the woods.

Kirby watched out the doorway until the truck could be seen or heard no more, when she turned her attention back to the living room, specifically the couch where Matt now sat waiting. He patted the cushion next to him in invitation.

She hesitated, then walked over with reluctant steps, on the one hand afraid he wanted to take up exactly where they'd left off and on the other hand afraid he didn't.

Matt said nothing when she sat at the opposite end of the couch, but she could tell the action bewildered him. They exchanged barely two words before he stretched, yawned and muttered something about the late hour and wanting to get an early start on his book first thing tomorrow morning.

Taking that as a definite *no longer interested,* Kirby made short work of sweeping up the hair she'd trimmed earlier that evening. While she did that, Matt put the chair back in the kitchen. When he reentered the living room, Kirby murmured a hasty good-night and headed straight for her bedroom, only to halt abruptly when Matt caught her wrist, pulled her right back into his arms and kissed her soundly.

The earth shifted beneath Kirby's feet, and at once she knew that she was wrong: Matt was still interested...very. She also knew that if she encouraged him in the least, she would not sleep alone this night.

Aching for his touch and frightened by the intensity of her need, Kirby eased free of his embrace and put precious inches between them.

"Good night, Matt," she said.

"Good night," he murmured, clearly disappointed. "Sweet dreams."

Doubtful that she would sleep, much less dream, Kirby escaped to the sanctuary of her cold, empty bed.

Chapter Eight

Once there, Kirby huddled under the quilts and tried yet again to take stock of her feelings for Matt.

Is this love? she agonized. Or just sex? Had she inherited some wanton gene from her man-crazy mother, a gene that could prove her ruination if she weren't careful?

Kirby had always feared such might be the case and tried so very hard to walk the straight and narrow, dragging her reluctant sister along behind. Now that Madison had grown up and taken a sharp detour to happiness, Kirby couldn't help but wonder if the time had come for big sis to take one, too.

So many new sensations thrilled her body...so many. And her lonely heart ached for love. But was love what Matt offered? Or...again...just sex?

Too inexperienced with men to know or even guess, Kirby buried her head under her pillow, as though she could hide from her troubles. She quickly discovered the futility of that exercise, of course, and came up for air, her thoughts once again on Matt and what she would do if yet another miracle happened and he actually wanted more than a holiday fling.

They had nothing in common, after all. Though dedicated to his craft, Matt was clearly undisciplined. And though very sweet and normal at times, he obviously enjoyed living life in the fast lane—the shoulders of which Kirby had traveled, the perils of which she knew quite well.

As for Matt's offering more than a holiday fling . . . Kirby almost laughed aloud at that foolishness. The Clints and Matts of this world weren't interested in long-term commitment, and the only reason he'd shown any interest in her tonight was because he'd worked hard and wanted a breather. Tomorrow would undoubtedly find him submerged in his book once more, their romantic idyll as long forgotten as a ten-minute coffee break.

And that, Kirby realized, was exactly what she feared most.

Christmas Eve began with new snow and a sudden plunge in temperature as the long-predicted Arctic cold front finally moved through the state. Kirby woke several hours later to the howls of a winter storm and the sound of Matt scooting back his chair in the kitchen.

She noted the time—7:00 a.m.—and pictured him settling himself in front of the word processor. Kirby knew she should be thrilled about his amazing turn-around, but felt nothing more than a great sense of loss. Obviously she'd drawn the right conclusions the night before. Break time was over; Kirby Lee Gibson could now take her foolish heart and crawl back up on the shelf.

Or under the covers, she thought, burrowing deeper into her pile of quilts. For once hating to face the day, she malingered. Her closed eyes stung with unshed tears of disappointment. Hating those silly tears and the sillier woman who shed them, Kirby tried to go back to sleep and find the sweet dreams Matt had wished for her not so many hours ago.

"Kirby?"

Matt's soft whisper barely penetrated her consciousness. Unsure if it was real or one of those elusive dreams, Kirby did not move or open her eyes.

"Oh, Kir-by."

The old wooden floor creaked with every step as he entered her room and slowly approached the bed. Suddenly the mattress dipped. No fantasy this, Kirby realized, instantly wide-awake with every hormone standing at attention.

She didn't have to turn over to know that Matt now sat on the bed beside her and much too close for comfort. To her dismay, he touched a hand to her flannel-encased shoulder, then trailed his fingers down her sleeve, searing a path clear to her beruffled wrist.

Kirby's pulse rate tripled.

Blushing, in no fit state to face him, she feigned sleep in hopes he'd leave.

But Matt didn't leave. He leaned over and pressed his lips to her neck—right above the telltale galloping pulse.

Kirby shot out of the bed, tangled her feet in the quilts and landed in a pitiful heap on the floor.

"Are you all right?"

Kirby looked up to find Matt sprawled on his stomach, peering down at her over the edge of the mattress. His eyes twinkled with merriment; his mouth twitched with suppressed laughter.

"What are you doing in here?" she demanded with as much dignity as she could muster.

"It's after seven. Aren't we going to exercise today?"

"Exercise!" Huffing and puffing her exasperation with long gowns, twisted bedclothes and baffling men, Kirby got painfully to her feet and busily smoothed her granny garb. "Since you're 'way past jumping jacks in the middle of the living-room floor,' just what kind of exercise did you have in mind?"

When Matt didn't respond, Kirby raised her gaze. She found his smile had vanished, and he now watched her intently with those breathtaking baby blues. At once she wished she hadn't phrased her question exactly that way.

"What are you looking at?" she snapped in embarrassment with a quick glance down at the pink flannel garment covering her from chin to toenail polish. Chaste, if anything, it certainly didn't deserve

that unmistakable gleam of desire that had replaced
the twinkle in his eye.

"Your gown," Matt replied, shifting position so
that he stretched out in *her* bed with his head resting
on *her* pillow. He crossed his arms over his chest and
shook his head slowly from side to side.

"And what's wrong with my gown?"

"Nothing. It's just not what I expected."

"You don't know me well enough to *expect* anything," Kirby said in irritation. "And for your information, flannel is perfect for a cabin with very little
heat."

"Ah. You bought the gown for this trip."

"Yes."

He nodded. "That explains it." He rubbed his chin
and made another lazy appraisal of her attire. "I'll bet
you usually sleep in silk or satin. Something with the
neck cut to here—" he pointed to the bottom of his
heart "—and with teeny tiny straps and maybe a slit
up the side."

Kirby caught her breath. "How did—?" Matt's
mischievous grin halted her. "I really don't think this
conversation is appropriate or necessary. Now, since
I was so rudely awakened, I may as well get up. Will
you please leave so I can get dressed?"

"Are we going to exercise?" he asked, sitting up to
swing his long legs over the side of her mattress. The
bedsprings squealed in protest, reminding Kirby of
another kind of exercise—an intimate, bedroom exercise for lovers.

"We are not."

He sighed. "Okay. We'll skip right to breakfast, then."

"I'm not hun—"

"Pecan waffles and maple syrup," Matt said, smiling as he added, "All made from one-hundred percent natural ingredients and *so-o-o* good for you," before striding from the room.

Forty-five minutes later found a disgracefully stuffed Kirby washing dishes in the kitchen. Close beside her stood Matt, who rinsed, dried and put away each piece of dinnerware as she handed it to him.

"There," she said, pulling the plug to drain the sudsy water. "All finished. You can get to work."

"Later," Matt said. "Right now I'm going to go sit by the fire. This cabin is downright chilly today." He walked toward the door, halting before he exited the room. "Coming?"

Surprised by the invitation—another coffee break already?—Kirby let her gaze travel the length of him from neatly trimmed hair to snakeskin boots. Her heart swelled with something suspiciously like love as she took special note of his chest-hugging Western shirt and his jeans, faded to pale blue in the most interesting places. Only a fool would have to be asked twice, she thought, trailing him all the way to the fireplace before the irony of that noun hit home.

A fool? Yes . . . and a big one.

After years of avoiding the wrong kind of man, it seemed that she'd now gone and fallen for one. And "wrong kind of man" that he was, *he'd* be the fool not to take advantage of her susceptibility if he found out.

Or maybe he already knew. Maybe she'd given herself away last night—even though she hadn't yet realized the state of her heart then.

There was a very good chance, Kirby realized, and downright wary of Matt's motives by the time she seated herself on the couch, Kirby actually flinched when he sat beside her and laid his arm across the back of it.

"Are you scared of me?" Matt asked, frowning. So much for his big plans to finish what the two of them had started the night before. He and Kirby might well have been strangers—a distressing development considering what good friends they'd become. Now it looked as though he was back to square one.

"Don't be silly," Kirby retorted even as she scooted over a tad and as good as confirmed his worst fears.

Not sure of the reason for her nervousness—was she dreading a continuation of their romantic idyll or wishing for one?—Matt decided to give her some space.

After hours spent soul-searching in the dark of night, he'd finally concluded he loved Kirby Lee Gibson. And with the dawn had come the realization that he wanted to spend his eternity with her.

Surely he could spare an hour...more, if necessary...of that eternity to help his lady love reach the same conclusions.

And if she didn't—if her prejudices got the best of her—he'd simply have to tell her the truth about his playboy image. So what if he never knew the blessing of unconditional love? So what if he lost both his publishers? Nothing mattered now but Kirby.

"That tree of ours is just about the prettiest one I've ever seen," he commented to steer the conversation to a subject designed to give her some insight as to what he was really like. "And believe you me, I've seen some pretty ones. My mom goes all out for Christmas—always has."

"Where do your parents live?"

"Yakima, Washington," Matt replied. "In an oversize Victorian house. It's kind of like this cabin... been in the family for years."

"And speaking of families... how does yours feel about your writing?" She tucked her feet up under her and turned slightly to sit sideways on the couch, her cheek resting on the back of the sofa, her hair tickling his hand.

"I think they're resigned to it now. Dad wasn't exactly thrilled when I started out, though."

"How old were you?"

"Eighteen and fresh out of high school," Matt replied. His head filled with memories, momentarily distracting him from his purpose. "You should have seen my ol' man's face when I told him I planned to major in journalism at the university. I'll never forget it."

"What did he want you to do?" Kirby's soft question brought him back.

"Coach football." Absently Matt wrapped a strand of her spun golden hair around and around his finger. "He played pro, you know. And he was damned good. Unfortunately I never was." He laughed without humor. "I've always felt bad about that. In fact, I created Ross Elliot as a sort of consolation prize for my dad. He loved adventure stories and macho heroes.''

"Are you saying you don't?" She sounded surprised.

"They're okay, I guess. Heaven knows I've made a buck or two off them. I really prefer another kind of hero, though. Someone with a little sensitivity."

Kirby sputtered with laughter. "I can't believe you're saying this to me."

"Why not?" he asked, affronted in spite of himself.

"Because of who and what you are. Sensitivity? Give me a break!"

"I resent that. You're obviously basing your opinion of me solely on the so-called *news flashes* of the tabloids. And why anyone would buy that garbage in the first place is beyond me."

"I don't buy them," Kirby retorted. "I read them in the checkout line at the grocery store. You're front-page news, Matt Foxx, and every single headline can't be wrong."

So much for hinting at his true nature without telling all. Clearly it was time for plan B: true confessions. Matt opened his mouth to defend his honor and spill his guts. "Sure you can. And I'm living proo—"

"Listen!" She put a hand to his lips and sat very still, obviously listening for something. "Do we have company?"

Not again.

Ready to murder that busybody Walter Williams, Matt jumped up and charged to the window. But it wasn't Walter who maneuvered his vehicle through the blizzard to the cabin.

It was somebody else. . . .

Matt frowned, watching a bright red truck pull to a halt in the front yard beside Kirby's snow-banked car, not three feet from the front porch.

By now Kirby stood next to him, and they watched in silence as two people, both swathed from head to toe in winter wraps, got out of the vehicle and trudged their way.

"Madison! It's Madison!" Kirby suddenly squealed, throwing back the door and dashing out onto the porch and then right on into the snow.

Immediately Matt recognized the pair.

Well, hell.

Matt watched Kirby embrace her sister. Both women laughed and talked at once, a sight that should have warmed his tender heart.

Instead, it ached. Would *he* ever be on the receiving end of Kirby's love? he wondered, stepping outside. Would he ever come home to her waiting arms, her joy, her love?

Deliberately Matt dragged his gaze from Kirby and Madison to another silent onlooker—Jason. But Matt found that Jason's eyes were not on his wife and sister-in-law. They were on him.

"Hello, there," Jason said with a nod.

"Hello, yourself," Matt responded.

Madison whirled at the sound of Matt's voice. "You're still here?" she blurted in obvious horror with a possessive glance toward her sister. Matt was reminded of a mama bear guarding her defenseless cubs.

So Madison read the tabloids, too, and now feared for Kirby's virtue. That rankled and suddenly Matt wanted to strangle them both, not to mention the man on whose shoulders lay seventy-five percent of the blame for his bad reputation. The other twenty-five percent was his own damned fault for cooperating all these years.

Obviously amused by his wife's open hostility, Jason looked right at Matt and gave him a broad wink. "No wonder I don't have my book yet," he commented with a chuckle. "I wouldn't write, either, if I was snowed in with a beautiful blonde."

"This is not funny!" Madison exploded, grabbing said blonde's hand and practically dragging her up the steps, across the porch and into the house.

Madison didn't halt until she reached the kitchen. She shut the door and whirled on Kirby. "What is going on here?"

"What is...?" Kirby saw red. "Ask your husband," she snapped. "He's the one who loaned Matt *our* cabin. Or did you tell him he could?"

"Of course I didn't, and he'll pay for that little mistake. Believe me, he'll pay. Now I want to know why you didn't send Matt packing the moment you found him here."

"Because he appealed to my professionalism, that's why. If anyone ever needed my expertise as an efficiency expert, this man does."

"Appealed to your 'professionalism,' my foot!" Madison exclaimed. "He appealed to something altogether different, and you know it. I demand to know exactly what the two of you have been doing all alone up here.''

Kirby's jaw dropped. Could this be the same sister who had once told her to mind her own business?

"I'm waiting..." Madison said, crossing her arms over her chest and impatiently tapping her booted toe on the linoleum floor.

"And you'll still be waiting this time next year," Kirby tartly informed her. Deliberately she changed the subject. "What are you doing here, anyway? You told me you were spending Christmas in Vermont."

To Kirby's astonishment, Madison burst into tears and caught her up in another hug. "We did go," she sobbed, "but I just couldn't get the spirit. I needed my big sis."

"Oh, Madison," Kirby said, adding her tears to her sister's, hugging her back.

Several moments passed before either could speak. Then Madison set Kirby away and wiped her eyes. "I'm so sorry I almost made you spend Christmas all alone."

"You have your own life to live," Kirby replied. "And besides, I'm not alone."

Madison put her fingertips to her temples, as though she had a headache. "Please don't remind me. I nearly died when Jason told me Matt was up here."

"And when was that?"

Madison nodded. "Right after I told *him* I'd changed my mind and wanted to spend Christmas out here with you. Boy, did I let him have it. Imagine him loaning our cabin to that—that *Romeo* without asking, and to top it all off, he wasn't a bit worried about you being here all alone with him. Not a bit! I guess he figured a womanizer like Matt wouldn't give you a second look.''

''Well, I like that!'' Kirby exclaimed, even though Madison's words merely reinforced her own doubts and fears.

''It's not that you're unattractive,'' Madison hastened to explain. ''I'm simply saying you have too much up here—'' she pointed to her head ''—and not enough down here—'' She pointed to her bosom. ''At least for Matt's tastes. And now that I think about it, *that's* probably the reason Jason wasn't worried. He knows you're much too sensible to fall for such a smooth operator.''

Kirby winced at that and said nothing, actions apparently not lost on her sister, who tensed.

''You *didn't* fall for him, *did you?*''

''Of course not,'' Kirby said, crossing her fingers behind her back to neutralize the fib.

Unfortunately Madison wasn't fooled. ''Kirby Lee Gibson, are you lying to me? Are you in love with this guy?''

''Don't be silly,'' Kirby replied, moving toward the door and escape from her sister's inquisition.

Madison immediately grabbed Kirby's shoulders to hold her immobile, then gazed into her eyes, window to the soul beyond. Kirby squirmed under the intense assessment and was not surprised when Madison's own eyes rounded in shock.

''Oh, my gosh, you are!'' Madison declared. *''You are!''* Whirling, she lunged for the door. ''I'm going to murder him!''

Chapter Nine

Kirby threw herself in front of her outraged sister and blocked the door with her body. "Oh, no, you won't. You'll mind your own business. I'm a grown woman, Madison. I can fight my own battles."

"Ah, but will you?" Madison retorted. "Or have you already surrendered?"

"Depends on what you mean by surrendered, I guess."

"Have you slept with Matt Foxx?" Madison asked, getting right to the point.

"I have not," Kirby replied, silently thanking her lucky stars she didn't have to lie.

"You swear?"

"I swear."

"Thank heaven for small favors!" Madison exclaimed, sinking into one of the kitchen chairs as though her knees wouldn't support her a moment longer. "I couldn't bear the thought of your wasting your precious love on that awful man."

"Matt is not 'awful,'" Kirby argued, words that surprised her as much as they seemed to surprise Madison. "In fact, he's really very kind, delightfully sentimental and surprisingly considerate."

Hadn't he saved the fox, put up a real Christmas tree *and* cooked?

"Oh, honey," Madison moaned in visible impatience. "It's time to wake up and smell the coffee...even if you don't drink it. Why, barely six months ago *Tattle Tale* magazine ran a picture of him out with the brand-new wife of a very influential man. You call that kind...sentimental...considerate?" She shook her head. "Don't kid yourself. Any good characteristics Matt might have—and there can't be many—could never outweigh the bad ones. I'm sure he's an embarrassment to Jason's publishing firm. Why, I'll bet they would drop him in a New York minute if he weren't so popular with readers."

Kirby sighed as the probable truth of those words sank home. "In my heart of hearts, I know you're right," she admitted, pulling out a chair and straddling it backward so she could face her sister. "But we've had such a nice time this week that I can't help but have doubts."

"Doubts? Honestly. I know love is blind, but this is ridiculous. The man is a skirt chaser to the nth degree. Why, I'll bet his little black book is thicker than the unabridged dictionary."

If Kirby hadn't been so upset by the truth of her sister's love-is-blind lecture, she would have laughed at this unexpected role reversal. Mere months ago she'd delivered the very same lecture to Madison, who had listened, calmly agreed to the logic of it and then eloped with Jason.

Well, Kirby wouldn't act so foolishly. If Walter's visit hadn't been enough to put her back in touch with reality, Madison's arrival and subsequent lecture certainly had.

Obviously she'd been kidding herself... probably due to the lethal mix of her innocence and Matt's experience. But now that she saw the truth and had her head back on straight, she intended to send Matt packing—exactly what she should have done the moment she found him in the cabin.

"So you've been cooped up here with my dear sister-in-law since Friday." Sprawled in the chair, Jason stuck a match into the bowl of his pipe to light the aromatic tobacco he'd just taken such pains to pack inside it. "That must have been a bummer."

"Actually I've enjoyed our time together," Matt told him, resting an elbow on the mantel. He gazed into the fireplace at the new log he'd just tossed there. "Kirby's been a big help to me, and the book's almost finished, thanks to her."

"Kirby's helping you write the Cairo story?" Jason asked with frown.

"That's right. She's given me a great idea for the scenes with Lola."

Jason hooted with laughter. "Are you trying to make me believe that you and Miss Priss researched those hot sex scenes? Give me a break, Matt. I'm the guy who invented your playboy image, remember? And not only do I know *you*, I know *her*."

"I'm not talking about the *love* scenes," Matt snapped, not for the first time vastly irritated with his pretentious publisher. "I'm talking about Lola's helping Ross solve his case. And would you just lay off Kirby? I like her—"

"What do you mean Lola's helping Ross solve his case?" Jason exploded, leaping to his feet. *"Have you lost your mind?"*

"Relax. It's a great plot twist."

"Plot twist?" Jason groaned dramatically. "For crying out loud, man. Haven't you ever heard that ol' saying about not fixing something that isn't broken?"

"But this plot was broken," Matt argued. "And now Kirby's idea has fixed it." He smiled reassuringly at his agitated companion. "Would you at least reserve judgment until you've read the book? I swear you're going to love what we've done."

Obviously still doubtful, Jason sank into the chair again. He sat in thoughtful silence for a moment, studying Matt intently as he puffed on his pipe. "Exactly what do you mean when you say you 'like' Kirby?"

Matt hesitated, caught unawares by the question. "I mean that I like her... a lot, in fact. She's a good woman."

Jason arched an eyebrow. "Good as in goody-two-shoes?"

"No," Matt told him. "Good as in good-hearted, a good time and good for the soul."

"Aw, man," Jason groaned. "Don't do this to me."

"Do what?"

"Fall for her. I've worked damned hard to create the Matt Foxx millions of readers love to hate. I've paid models, tipped off the press and bribed photographers to snap shots that look as though you're out all alone with some sexy *married* lovely instead of in a group. Hell, I've even lied to my own wife, who couldn't keep a secret if her life depended on it. You can't undo all that by falling for an ordinary woman like Kirby."

"For your information, Kirby is *extra*ordinary," Matt exploded, striding over to glare down at Jason. "And more woman than any of those bimbos you've lined up for me."

Jason's gaze narrowed. "All this is too late, isn't it?" he muttered in obvious disbelief. "You're already in love with her."

Matt almost denied the accusation, then decided against it. He *was* in love with Kirby, and Jason might as well get used to the fact that there would be no more manipulation of the Foxx reputation.

"Yes. I am."

Jason groaned like a man in mortal pain. "That new book of yours had better be a winner, Matt, because *this* foolishness will surely be the death of your career."

Matt opened his mouth to argue that good writing and not good PR had resulted in his bestsellers, but never got the chance.

"What foolishness?" Madison demanded from the kitchen door. Matt whirled to the sound of her voice, his heart in his throat. His gaze locked with that of Kirby, who stood right behind her sister. Had she heard his confession? he wondered, anxiously trying to gauge her expression.

She looked tense and maybe just a little irritated, neither of which were reactions Matt had hoped the revelation of his love for her would bring.

"Matt's affair with your sister, that's what foolishness," Jason said, yanking Matt's attention away from Kirby. Struck dumb by Jason's choice of words, Matt could only gape at the publisher. "I can already smell the smoke from his image, not to mention career, going up in flames."

"Affair!" Madison exploded before Matt could recover enough to respond to his publisher's outrageous comment. "Kirby would never get involved with the likes of *him*. Never." She gave Matt a go-to-hell look so potent he broke out in a sweat.

Silence followed Madison's harsh declaration. Kirby realized that *she* was now on the receiving end of Matt's stare and decided he must be waiting for her to deny Madison's statement. But why should she? He'd obviously been bragging to Jason that the two of them were having an affair.

Clearly her worst suspicions about him were right, and the sooner he left the cabin, the better.

One minute of silence stretched into two. Outside, the wind whistled around the cabin, wrapping it in a chilly blanket. Inside, the fire crackled and bravely fought back the chill.

Kirby noted that Matt next shifted his gaze to Jason, whose face at once flushed scarlet. Jason squirmed, ran a finger around the inside of his collar as though it choked him, then turned to his wife. "Ladies, I think it's time I—"

"No!" Matt snapped, cutting off whatever it was Jason had started to say.

"But this whole thing is—" Jason began.

"Shut up!" Matt growled, coming abruptly to life. Two steps closed the distance to the bunk beds, from where he retrieved his suitcase with a yank. He tossed it to the floor and haphazardly threw all manner of clothes and shoes into it.

Kirby noted his flushed cheeks, the hard set of his jaw. Though she'd anticipated anger, a logical reaction since she'd foiled his plans, she now sensed another emotion altogether. It was almost as though she'd hurt him....

At once confused, she took a step forward. "Matt?"

Immediately Madison caught her arm. "Let him go, Kirby. You need a three-piece-suit, nine-to-five sort of guy who can give you the stability you've always craved. Matt's...well, he's just not your type."

Matt stopped packing and pivoted to face Madison, his sharp gaze nailing her to the wall. She raised her chin in defiance and glared right back at him.

Jason groaned. "Madi, we really need to tal—"

Matt silenced him with a look this time. "I'd rather not move the computer, if you don't mind. Do you think you could leave word with Walter when you clear out of here? I'll finish the book then. You'll have it on your desk by mid-January."

"I, uh, sure, sure." Belatedly Jason glanced toward his wife and shrugged rather sheepishly. "If you girls agree, of course."

"That's fine with us," Madison said.

Matt stood in silence for a moment, his eyes on Kirby. Though aching to stop him, she said nothing.

Madison had spoken the truth when she said Kirby needed stability in her life. Matt was not stability. Matt was spontaneity, excitement, fun . . . traits her mother would have loved . . . traits Kirby had learned to fear.

Matt reached for his coat. He slipped it on, and after a last look around, headed for the kitchen.

"I'll help you clear the snow off your car," Jason said. Snatching up his coat, he followed Matt. Kirby heard their footfall on the kitchen floor, heard the back door open and then shut. Minutes later Matt's vehicle roared to life and he drove right out of hers.

"The tree is really pretty," Madison commented several hours later from where she sat curled up on one end of the sofa, cup of steaming hot chocolate in hand. Strangely silent, Jason sat at the other end, sipping on black coffee. "I'm surprised you put up a real one. I didn't think you liked them."

"I don't," Kirby responded. "The tree was Matt's idea. We walked all through the woods to find it, and—" Abruptly Kirby halted, her head filled with vivid memories of that day. "I'm sorry he isn't going to get to enjoy it," she lamely concluded, avoiding their sympathetic gazes.

"His leaving *was* for the best," Madison softly reminded her.

"I realize that," Kirby replied.

"You two are total opposites," Madison continued.

"I know."

"He's a womanizer, a rounder, a party animal."

At that, Jason choked on his coffee. Coughing and sputtering, he set his mug on the end table.

Madison leaned over and pounded his back, obviously concerned. "Are you okay?"

"Fine," he told her. Abruptly he got to his feet and walked over to Kirby's chair. Leaning down, he placed a hand on each armrest and looked her right in the eye. "For what it's worth, I apologize for my part in this. I'd never have sent him up here if I'd known you were coming." Jason straightened and glanced back at his wife as though he still had something on his mind. Then he sighed and shook his head. "Want me to go get our suitcases out of the truck?"

"Please," Madison said. "And get the presents, too." She turned to Kirby the moment Jason disappeared outside. "I made him bring the ones you mailed plus several more." She chuckled. "You should have seen us at the airport trying to load everything into the cab of that truck we rented. Thank goodness we ran into some friends who'd flown out to ski at Teton Pass. They were a big help. Don and Carol Patterson . . . do you know them?"

"No."

"They invited us to stay at their lodge about fifteen miles from here. We're thinking we might go after Christmas. I do love to ski, and Carol said you could come, too, so it's not like we'd be deserting you or anything."

When Kirby, who also loved to ski, did not so much as smile in response, Madison's own smile faded away.

"You'll be over him before you know it," she promised. Then, in another abrupt role reversal, she hesitantly added, "Won't you?"

"I'm over him now," Kirby bravely lied, reassuming her proper position as mother figure. Madison had flown and driven many miles to spend Christmas with her. Kirby would be less than gracious if she let her broken heart ruin their brief time together. "And skiing sounds wonderful. This is going to be the best Christmas ever, just you wait and see."

"Yeah?" Madison asked. Her troubled eyes told Kirby she wasn't so sure.

"Yeah. We'll start by making cookies. Remember those little white ones Nana used to make every Christmas Eve? They looked like snowballs."

"Mmm, yes." Clearly excited, Madison swung her feet to the floor. "Do you have the recipe?"

"It should be in that wooden box with all the others," Kirby said, rising from her chair to join her sister.

Arm in arm, they walked to the kitchen, stopping at the door when Jason burst into the room in a swirl of cold air and misguided snowflakes, arms laden with suitcases and shopping bags.

"Drop those right there and come on," Madison called out to him, beckoning. "We're going to make snowball cookies."

To Kirby's surprise—he didn't seem like a snowball-cookie kind of guy—Jason did exactly that. And though she didn't really want him around, she resolved to make an extraspecial effort to get along...for the sake of the season, for the sake of this sister she loved so dearly.

During the next two hours Kirby and Madison mixed, shaped and baked the cookies. Then Jason rolled them in confectioners' sugar and carefully placed them in a tin decorated with a Currier and Ives scene that was not one bit more beautiful than the view outside their window.

Madison sang carols in her sweet soprano as they worked and occasionally succeeded in coaxing her husband and sister into harmonizing. When they weren't singing, Jason shared stories of Christmases past.

He came from a large family, and his traditional upbringing came as a pleasant surprise to Kirby, as did his plans to carry on those traditions with the bride he so obviously treasured.

Kirby saw him through new eyes before they finished their baking. And though she still harbored some reservations about his and Madison's future together, she felt better about it than ever before. As a result, she actually warmed to him, a miracle evidently not lost on Madison.

Clearly pleased that the two people she loved most had actually spent time together without locking horns, she fairly danced around the kitchen in her excitement.

Her mood was contagious. Kirby caught and held on to it until bedtime, when she spread a couple of extra quilts on the bunk Matt had vacated. Too tired to bother changing the linens, she crawled under the covers the minute Madison and Jason retreated to the bedroom around eleven-thirty.

Instantly her smile vanished and her good spirits flew right up the chimney with the soot and smoke. At once struggling with the gloom she'd somehow held at bay all afternoon, Kirby burrowed under the blankets and buried her face in the pillow.

The smell of Matt's after-shave suddenly assaulted her senses, and she missed him with an ache the likes of which she'd never known, the likes of which no drug and maybe not even time could ever relieve.

Five miles down the winding, snow-covered highway, Matt endured a similar ache. He sat alone in a bedroom in Walter's living quarters over his country store, a room the old man had rented for ten dollars and an autograph.

Matt stared at a tiny black-and-white television, on which flickered the images of *Miracle on Thirty-fourth Street,* the old movie he and Kirby both loved. He thought back to the conversation they'd had about miracles and realized there would not be one on Gibson Ridge this Christmas.

That fact saddened him and obliterated any lingering remains of his holiday spirit. With a sigh of regret and a flick of the wrist, Matt turned off the television and got to his feet, intending to take a quick shower and go to bed.

He opened his suitcase and dug through the contents for some clean clothes, but found only a pair of dress pants and a crisp white shirt that he'd packed for some unknown reason. All his other clothes, though neatly folded and carefully placed into the suitcase by Kirby days ago, had been worn already and most of them more than once.

Matt reached for a pair of the jeans anyway, then decided he might as well make use of Walter's Laundromat facilities, situated between his general store and the twenty-four-hour café where Matt had eaten a surprisingly good dinner that evening.

Matt knew there were some video games there. What better way to spend Christmas Eve? he wondered gloomily as he bundled up his laundry and headed down the rickety stairs.

Mere minutes later he ducked under a sprig of mistletoe someone had tacked over the doorway and admitted there were definitely better ways to spend one's holiday... kissing the woman he loved, among them.

Unfortunately such a possibility was now very remote, he realized as he routinely searched the pockets of his jeans for coins or anything else that might damage the washing machine.

He found several pennies, a dime, a paper clip and... a pair of pink bikini panties.

At once overwhelmed with the enormity of his loss, Matt fought the tears ''real men'' never cried. He decided those men hadn't loved and lost Kirby Lee Gibson.

Why, oh, why was she so eager to believe the worst? he asked himself for the thousandth time, though he well knew the answer: her tragic childhood. He then acknowledged it wasn't the *why* that concerned him so much as the *how*. To his way of thinking, he'd more than proved he wasn't the reckless writer of the tabloids.

So how could Kirby ignore the facts he'd presented? How could she refuse to give him a chance to prove his worth?

And how, *how* would he ever change her mind?

Chapter Ten

Christmas Day dawned clear and bright. Kirby peeked out the window the moment she woke and found a sparkling fairyland of snow and ice.

This was indeed a white Christmas worthy of the songwriter's dreams. Unfortunately Kirby's own enthusiasm for it seemed to have followed Matt out the door.

Vowing that neither Madison nor Jason would discover the extent of her blues, Kirby pasted a smile on her face and dressed in red pants and a bright green sweatshirt decorated with reindeer, a jam-packed sleigh and a ho-ho-hoing Santa Claus. Around her neck she hung a gold bell suspended from a red satin ribbon. From her ears she dangled identically beribboned bells, these in miniature.

Kirby next brushed her hair and then pulled it back in a ponytail, which she tied with yet another red ribbon. Feeling a lot like one of those gaily decorated Christmas packages now stashed under the tree and waiting to be opened, Kirby headed for the kitchen to make hot chocolate.

Madison joined her there just in time to garnish the steaming mugs with marshmallows. Jason entered the room moments later and surprised both women by pouring himself a cup of the chocolate instead of his usual black coffee.

Both Jason and Madison watched her anxiously as they all moved to the living room and seated themselves on the floor at the foot of the lighted tree. Highly conscious of their concern, Kirby smiled, laughed and otherwise faked her way through the ritual of opening gifts.

Only once did she feel any real emotion: when she opened the very last present under the tree. It was one Madison had brought for her—a photograph album filled with pictures of Kirby, Madison and their precious nana.

Madison explained that she'd found the forgotten snapshots in a box the day of their grandmother's funeral. She had smuggled them away, and later selected the best to be mounted in the album as a gift for the big sister who had sacrificed her childhood so Madison could have one.

Touched to the heart by the gesture, Kirby burst into tears for the second time since Madison's arrival the day before. And once those tears began to fall, she could not stop them.

"I-I'm sorry," she stammered between sobs. "I don't know what's wrong with me."

"It's not a what, but a who," Madison said with a sniff of sympathy. "And I'd love to get my hands on him right about now. This whole thing is all his fault."

"No," Jason muttered. "It's all my fault, and in more ways than you know. But I'm going to make things right as soon as possible." He stood and reached down to pull his baffled wife to her feet. "I owe you an apology, Madi, and I owe Kirby an explanation. Unfortunately I'm not free to give either just yet. I will say that I believe Kirby needs to do some serious soul-searching and have a long heart-to-heart with Matt before she shuts him out of her life for good. For that reason, you—" he pointed to his wife "—and I are getting the hell out of here so she can do exactly that."

"But where are you going?" Kirby demanded, scrambling to stand.

"Teton Pass," he replied. "We have friends waiting there."

"I can't leave Kirby here all alone," Madison argued.

"If she has any sense at all, she won't be alone," Jason replied with a stern look in Kirby's direction. "And I promise we'll be back by New Year's Eve." With that, he hustled his wife off to the bedroom. Several minutes later the two of them emerged with their suitcases.

Kirby handed them their just-opened gifts, which she'd carefully packed into a box.

"This is probably a waste of effort," she told her brother-in-law. "Even if I get up the nerve to talk to Matt, he might not be willing to talk to me."

"He *is* stubborn, for a fact," Jason said. "But he's also as smitten as you are—"

"He is?" Kirby interjected in surprise.

"Absolutely," Jason promised with a brisk nod. "So he'll probably be willing, maybe even eager, to talk with you. Just to make sure, though, Madi and I'll stop by Walter's on our way out and tell Matt the coast will be clear by lunchtime. That'll give you a few hours to get yourself together before he comes back to the cabin."

"Are you sure you know what you're doing?" Madison asked Jason with a worried frown.

"Damned sure," her husband replied. "Trust me."

Apparently Madison did. With a shrug of resignation and a sigh of bewilderment, she gave her sister a brief hug, then moved toward the door. "We'll only be a half hour away. I left the number on the dresser."

"I don't have a phone," Kirby reminded her, hastily adding, "But I won't need one, anyway," when Madison's frown immediately returned.

Madison turned to Jason. "When am I going to get the explanation that's supposed to make me feel better about all this?"

"As soon as we get in the truck," he replied.

"Then by all means, let's go."

Moments later Kirby stood on the porch and waved goodbye to the occupants of the gleaming red truck lurching its way through the arch of trees to the highway.

At once the solitude of the cabin closed in on her. She walked to the fireplace, put another log on the dying blaze and then settled herself under an afghan on the couch nearby.

Purposefully she relived every companionable moment with Matt, every conversation, every passionate kiss. She then recalled each and every article she'd ever read about him and came to the conclusion that the facts simply did not add up.

The Matt Foxx she knew could not be the devil-may-care playboy of the tabloids. He was a spontaneous, fun-loving, family-oriented man, whose appearance had changed her life irrevocably. She could never go back to the mundane existence she used to cherish. And no ordinary man would ever satisfy her again.

But would an ordinary woman satisfy Matt? What if she was wrong and all those stories really were true? Why, he could have any female he wanted. Why on earth would he settle for a plain Jane such as Kirby Lee Gibson? And if he could settle, would her love be enough to keep him at home and happy?

Kirby believed it could, and decided it all came to this. She could do the sensible thing, the safe thing, and live her life alone and lonely. Or she could do something she had never done before: take a risk that just might result in the happiness of her wildest dreams.

Never one to gamble—and that in spite of years lived within shouting distance of a casino—Kirby nonetheless knew that this time she had to trust her instincts enough to place a bet on a couple of less-than-sure things . . . Matt's character and his love for her.

And if her eagerness to wager wasn't proof she was no longer the same woman who'd arrived at the cabin Friday night, Kirby simply didn't know what was.

Excited, fearful, she slipped into her coat and went outside to move her car around back so Matt wouldn't spot it on his arrival and leave before she could explain her fears and apologize for her lack of faith in him. After sending heavenward a prayer that Matt would park his truck in front of the cabin this time, she stepped back inside to plan a reception he would never forget.

Matt guided his vehicle the last few feet to the cabin and braked within five feet of the front porch. He killed the engine and sat for a moment in indecision, seriously considering abandoning his book and following Kirby to Cheyenne.

In the end he decided against that course of action. After all, Kirby had made it quite clear she would not be happy to see him.

Why she and the Lawrences had cut their holiday so short, Matt couldn't imagine. But it didn't matter, anyway, he realized, since the end result was the same. He still had five chapters left to write on a book that had been nothing but trouble from day one.

And now he had no Kirby around to inspire him.

With little enthusiasm, Matt stepped out of the truck and stomped his way to the front porch. He opened the door, welcoming the warmth left over from a fire not long dead. After tossing a fresh log in the grate, Matt struck a match and ignited it.

Only after the blaze took hold did he slip out of his coat. Matt then walked over to the tree, still standing and decorated, and took note of the telltale bits of paper and ribbon strewn about the floor under it. This evidence of Kirby's merry Christmas only served to compound his misery.

Matt closed his eyes, backtracking through some recent memories to the night he met Kirby. In spite of himself, he smiled, vividly recalling the scene. He remembered his initial fear upon discovering he had a visitor and his subsequent surprise when said visitor suddenly serenaded him with "White Christmas."

Why, he could almost hear her now....

No... he *could* hear her now... loud, clear and delightfully off-key. Heart suddenly pounding with excitement, Matt rushed to the bedroom. He stumbled to a halt just inside the door, his gaze riveted to Kirby, who smiled shyly at him from where she sat crosslegged on the bed.

Dressed from chin to ankle in, of all things, his forgotten long johns, she was a sight to behold, and it was all Matt could do not to grab her up in his arms.

Why is she here? he wondered, masking his joy with difficulty. Had Jason blabbed the truth in spite of his promise not to? Did mild-mannered, borderline-dull Matt Foxx now meet Kirby's rigid standards regarding suitable dates?

At once old suspicions, old disappointments and old hurts returned.

Sensing emotion that could only mean Matt was not as glad to see her as she'd hoped, Kirby scrambled off the bed and lunged for her clothes.

So much for impetuosity. Clearly she'd made a drastic mistake and a fool of herself in the bargain.

He did not want a plain Jane after all.

Clothes in hand, she turned . . . and ran smack into Matt's waiting arms. Totally humiliated, she shook off his belated embrace, ignored his stammered explanation and dashed to the haven of the bathroom. With a click of the lock, she made sure he would not follow.

Another click of that lock demolished that idea and reminded her Matt remembered the trick she'd taught him. A heartbeat later he burst into the room. Kirby squealed and threw her clothes at him, then lunged for the window, fully intending to crawl through it to freedom, exactly as she had once before.

She had no better success this time than last, however, and found herself swept up into Matt's arms and carried back into the bedroom, where he deposited her on the big iron bed.

"Sit," he said when she would have made another mad dash to escape.

Kirby sat, eyeing him warily when he joined her.

"Now I want to know what you're doing here," Matt said.

Looking deep into his sky blue eyes, Kirby read the same confusion she herself felt. Encouraged by it, she took a deep breath and one last, crazy gamble.

"I'm here because I love you."

Dead silence greeted that heartfelt admission, silence Kirby thought would never end. Finally Matt spoke. "Does Jason's big mouth have anything to do with this sudden protestation?"

"What are you talking about?" Kirby asked, as baffled as she was hurt by his cold reply.

"Jason didn't tell you about me?"

"Tell me what? *What?*" she demanded.

Afraid to hope, Matt once again fell silent. Either she was a wonderful actress or she honestly didn't know.... And if she didn't know, then she loved him in spite of his Matt Foxx reputation, not to mention in ignorance of his Dillon Mathias identity.

In fact, Matt realized with growing joy, Kirby probably loved the real Dillon Mathias Foxx—a man he barely knew himself.

"Kirby, I'm not what you think I am," he said, getting to his feet to pace the room. "All those stories you've read—the ones in the supermarket gossip rags—they're made up."

Clearly stunned, Kirby said nothing for a moment. Then she drew in a shaky breath. "But I saw the pictures of you and all those women."

"Carefully planned shots, every one of them." He sat beside her. "You can do anything with a camera, honey. Think of all the movies you've seen, think of the equipment that had to be all around those actors and actresses, the lights, the mikes, the cameras. Did you see them? No. But they were there, all the same."

Kirby's eyes widened as she contemplated his words in silence.

"I was always at a party or at least in a group when those photos were taken," Matt continued. "It was all one long publicity stunt, hatched by Jason when he first signed me on."

"But you're so talented your books would sell without the gimmick," Kirby argued, words that warmed Matt more than the crackling fire. "Why would you ever agree to a scam like that?"

He laughed softly. "Talented?" He shrugged. "Maybe. Insecure? *Absolutely*... and desperate to get published so I could prove my worth to my dad."

"By why keep up the charade all these years?" Kirby then asked, edging closer to gaze right into his eyes. "Surely it's upsetting to your family."

"Actually Dad is proud as punch when one of his buddies brings the latest issue of *Tattle Tale* or *Hot Stuff* to work. As for Mom, well, she's done her share of worrying, but she laughs about it now. Thank goodness she has a good sense of humor."

"But what about you? Aren't you embarrassed by all the notoriety?"

He shrugged. "I never minded all that much until I met you—probably because you're the first woman whose opinion mattered to me in a very long time."

"Oh, Matt," she whispered, her voice husky with emotion.

"And I get a little sick of the long-lost relatives who've crawled out of the woodwork to ask for loans. Unfortunately stories of my vast wealth have been greatly exaggerated, too."

"So you don't date a different woman every night of the week?" Kirby asked, evidently not the least bit concerned that he wasn't rolling in dough.

Matt grinned. "Are you kidding? I haven't had a real date in ages. Jason expects two books a year. Do you realize how many pages that is?"

"Yes," Kirby said. "But you write very fast once you get going. Why, you finished several chapters in a matter of hours. You could probably produce three or four books a year if you set your mind to it.''

"Actually I do produce that many." Matt heaved a sigh. "Kirby, I have another confession to make.''

"I'm not sure I can handle another one," she replied, but her eyes had begun to sparkle and a smile teased the corner of her full, kissable lips.

Matt gulped at the sight and struggled to remember what he had to say. "This confession has to do with those Skeeter Skunk stories you love.''

Kirby's smile vanished. "What about them?''

"Do you know who the author is?''

"Of course I do...Dillon Mathias." Her eyes bored into his. "Why do you ask?''

Matt ducked her stare and got to his feet. He walked over to the window, looked out and oh-so-casually replied, "Because he's me. Er, I'm him." Matt swallowed hard and tried again. "My given name is Dillon Mathias Foxx. Dillon is my mother's maiden name, Mathias is—''

"Arrgh!" Kirby screeched, cutting off the rest of Matt's explanation. He whirled at the sound...just in time for Kirby's boot to bounce off his chest. "How could you do this to me!" she exclaimed, scrambling for the other boot, no doubt intending to hurl it, too.

Matt lunged for her, and together they fell across the bed. Kirby landed on her back with Matt half on top of her, a position that did not hamper her ability to grab one of the feather pillows and heartily pound his head with it.

Matt yanked the pillow from her hands and tossed it to the floor. After sweeping the other one out of reach, he pinned Kirby's flailing arms over her head.

"Will you just stop?" he panted, honestly concerned that his latest bombshell had been one true confession too many for her.

"Why should I?" she retorted. "You deserve a little bodily harm for what you've put me through the last five days. Skeeter Skunk, indeed. No wonder you knew all about those books. You wrote them!"

"Please don't be upset," Matt pleaded. "I had my reasons for deceiving you."

"Want to share them with me?"

"Gladly," Matt murmured. "But I think we'd better move to the couch first."

"Why?"

"Because I have a penchant for sexy blondes in red long johns, and I'm having one hell of a time keeping my mind on my business and my hands to myself."

"Oh, Matt, forget the explanation. I want you to promise me that I'm the only blonde who'll ever wear these awful old things."

"You're the only one. The only one."

"Now tell me that you love me," she said, softly adding, "I told you."

"And those words were music to my ears," he admitted, lowering his head so he could plant a kiss on those irresistible lips of hers. "I love you, Kirby Lee Gibson. For now, for always."

"I love you, too, Matt. Or should I say Dillon Mathias Foxx?"

"'Matt' is fine. I'm only called all three when someone is angry with me. You're not angry with me, are you?"

"No."

"Bless you, honey. I'll spend the rest of my life making this up to you, I swear."

"I'm glad something good is going to come from all this deception," Kirby replied, slipping her hands free so she could lock her fingers behind Matt's neck. She tugged until he kissed her again, then purred her contentment, a sexy sound that shimmied down Matt's spine.

"Last call for the couch," he warned, his control now teetering on the brink of oblivion.

"Forget the couch," she replied. "We're doing fine right here."

"But I have one—no, two—other things I have to say."

"Please talk fast."

Matt did. "First of all, Jason doesn't know about Skeeter Skunk."

Kirby laughed with delight. "No wonder you were afraid to tell me the truth. Don't worry, he'll never hear it from me. Now, what's the second thing you have to say?"

"It's Christmas, and I haven't given you a present."

"Your love is the best gift of all," she said with a tender smile.

"All the same, I have something else. It's a promise, Kirby—straight from the heart, based on what I feel for you."

Kirby reached up to touch the tear snaking its way down Matt's cheek. "And what promise is that?" she asked, her own eyes shining with joy.

"The rest is the best, honey," he replied. "The rest is the best."

Epilogue

"Have I told you how sorry I am for all those awful things I said about you?" Madison leaned forward slightly when she asked the question, nearly squashing Kirby, who sat wedged between her and Matt in the truck.

The man Kirby loved to distraction took his eyes off the snowy road just long enough to give her a reassuring smile. "Several times, actually."

"And every time you do, he tells you to forget about it," Jason added with a chuckle from where he sat scrunched against the passenger door.

"Wipe that smile off your face," Madison snapped, punching him in the ribs. "I'd never have made such a fool of myself if you'd just been honest with me from the start."

"I know, I know," Jason replied, rubbing his side. "And if you'll recall, I've apologized for that at least as many times as you've apologized to Matt."

"So now that we're all forgiven, why don't we do what Matt suggested and forget?" Kirby asked with a huff of exasperation at the entire conversation, which had been ongoing since the moment Jason and Madison returned to the cabin that morning.

"Good idea," Matt agreed. "It's exactly ten minutes until the New Year. What better time for new beginnings?"

"No better time, I guess," Madison replied, wiggling her way back against the seat, a move that pushed Kirby closer to Matt.

Kirby didn't mind, of course, and took advantage of the situation by resting her cheek on his shoulder and snuggling up.

A sense of peace settled over her, and on its heels came new wonder at the miracles this Christmas had brought. Mere days ago she'd arrived on the mountain all alone. Now she sat surrounded by the people she cherished most in the world.

What more could any woman ask? she wondered.

"That steak I ate tonight was really delicious," Jason said, breaking into Kirby's thoughts. "How on earth you ever found that restaurant is beyond me. It looked like a real greasy spoon from the outside."

"And what about that club?" Madison reminded her husband. "Wasn't it a pleasant surprise?" She sighed softly, a wistful sound to Kirby's ear. "I do love to dance. Too bad we had to leave before they rang in the New Year. The hostess said they were going to have a really special celebration."

"What I've got planned for midnight will top anything they've got," Matt promised, exchanging a grin with Kirby.

"You mean we're not going back to the cabin yet?" Madison asked, perking right up.

"Nope," Matt told her.

"Then where *are* we going?" Jason asked.

"Another little place I've found," Matt said even as he activated the turn signal of his truck and headed it down a well-illuminated side street.

Jason laughed and shook his head. "For a man who claims to have spent the last two months stuck in a cabin in the woods, you sure do know Jackson well."

"Kirby and I did a little exploring when we came to town yesterday," Matt replied.

"I didn't realize you two ever left the cabin," Madison commented, clearly surprised.

"Just long enough to get the blood tests and the marriage license," Kirby told her sister with a wink at Matt.

Silence followed her answer, then Madison emitted an earsplitting screech of pure delight. *"You're getting married?"*

"That's right," Matt said. "And we're counting on the two of you to stand up with us." He guided the truck onto a paved parking area and pulled up in front of a small frame church with stained-glass windows and a tall steeple. Light streamed a warm welcome from those windows and formed a colorful pattern on the snow.

"Oh, honey," Madison whispered, throwing her arms around Kirby. "Of course we will."

"What, no lecture on the folly of short courtships?" Kirby teased when Madison released her. Anxiously she scanned her sister's smiling face, barely visible in the dark.

"From me? The woman who married the first man she ever dated, three weeks, two days and seven hours after she met him?" Madison laughed and hugged her sister again.

"Six and a half hours, actually," Jason corrected. He extended his hand to Matt over the heads of the women. "Welcome to the family. You're one lucky guy."

"I think so, too," Matt told him, shaking the proffered hand.

"Do you have rings?" Madison asked, suddenly all business.

Kirby nodded.

"What about your bridal bouquet?"

"Miniature poinsettias and a sprig of mistletoe. It's waiting inside the church."

"Music . . . we have no music!" Madison bounced the seat and its other three occupants in her agitation and excitement.

"I was hoping you'd help us out there," Kirby replied, sharing an amused glance with Matt. "You've had 'The Wedding March' memorized since you were twelve years old."

Madison giggled. "I have, haven't I? But what about Matt's family? Won't his mother and father be upset about missing their only son's wedding? And what about *his* nana? She sounded so much like ours when you told me about her. Won't she get her feelings hurt?''

''My mother and father barely survived my sisters' weddings. In fact, my dad tried to bribe both my brothers-in-law into eloping. As for Nana...trust me when I say she won't mind at all.''

''Then we're all set,'' Madison said as though she'd done all the planning for this ceremony that would be the culmination—or was it just the beginning?—of all Kirby's secret hopes and dreams.

''Aren't you forgetting one rather important requirement for a successful wedding?'' Jason asked, laughter in his voice.

''What's that?'' his wife asked.

''The preacher,'' Jason said.

''Oh, my gosh!'' Madison exclaimed. She turned to Kirby. ''Where on earth are you going to find a preacher this time of night?''

''He should be waiting inside the church,'' Kirby told her. She reached for Matt's watch, the hands of which glowed. ''And since he's expecting us promptly at midnight, I suggest we go in.''

''I can't believe you actually found a preacher willing to perform a midnight ceremony,'' Jason commented, opening his door and putting a foot to the ground so he wouldn't tumble right out.

''That's a miracle for sure,'' Madison blithely agreed, slipping off the seat into her husband's waiting arms.

Taking advantage of the moment alone in the truck, Kirby shared a quick hug and kiss with her husband-to-be.

"Luckily miracles have never been a problem for us," she then said to her sister and brother-in-law. "In fact . . . Matt and I specialize in them."

*   *   *   *   *

This is the season of giving, and Silhouette proudly offers you its sixth annual Christmas collection.

SILHOUETTE

Christmas Stories

1991

Experience the joys of a holiday romance and treasure these heartwarming stories by four award-winning Silhouette authors:

Phyllis Halldorson—"A Memorable Noel"
Peggy Webb—"I Heard the Rabbits Singing"
Naomi Horton—"Dreaming of Angels"
Heather Graham Pozzessere—"The Christmas Bride"

Discover this yuletide celebration—sit back and enjoy Silhouette's Christmas gift of love.

Take 4 bestselling love stories FREE
Plus get a FREE surprise gift!

NORA ROBERTS

Love has a language all its own, and for centuries, flowers have symbolized love's finest expression. Discover the language of flowers—and love—in this romantic collection of 48 favorite books by bestselling author Nora Roberts.

Starting in February 1992, two titles will be available each month at your favorite retail outlet.

In February, look for:

Irish Thoroughbred, Volume #1
The Law Is A Lady, Volume #2

Collect all 48 titles and become fluent in the Language of Love.

LOL192

THE LANGUAGE of LOVE